Davalynn Spencer

Wilson Creek Publishing

Print ISBN: 979-8-9907518-0-4
Ebook ISBN: 979-8-9907518-1-1

Cover design by ebooklaunch.com

For my thoughts are not your thoughts,
neither are your ways my ways, saith the LORD.
For as the heavens are higher than the earth,
so are my ways higher than your ways,
and my thoughts than your thoughts.

Isaiah 55:8-9

Dedicated to:

Harley the Wonder Horse

CHAPTER ONE

Cañon City, Colorado
September 1912

The back of Grace's neck prickled beneath her silk bandana.

She tugged her hat down and turned slowly from the livery hitch rail, Harley's reins in hand.

An automobile rumbled by with a buggy in its wake, and the feed store across the street yawned open, awaiting early customers. Behind it, only partially visible, stood her grandparents' parsonage —now a boarding house—neglected and mute.

Her gaze slid to the right, skimming below her brim along the lane that led to the river, cutting between the house and the first block of stores on Main Street. There—in the lane, a man and woman struggled.

He punched her and she fell.

Grace hit the saddle and charged.

With her left boot deep in Harley's side, she leaned to the right, arm poised.

Too late the attacker saw her, and she hooked him under the chin.

Harley slid to a stop, reared, and pawed the air.

The man screamed.

Grace tightened her arm around his throat. "You hit another woman and I'll turn this horse loose on you." She squeezed tighter. "You won't hit anyone ever again."

She let go and the cur slid to the ground. Crawling off on all fours, he glanced back through long yellow hair and swore.

She heeled Harley into a leaping charge.

The scoundrel kicked up and ran for the river, disappearing into the underbrush.

Harley's neck bowed as he blew and pranced, the charge and brief battle firing through his veins. "Good man." Grace patted his neck on both sides. "You saved the day again, ol' boy, but this time, for real."

She stepped off and led Harley back, then dropped his reins and knelt beside the woman.

"Please—" A ragged whisper. "Help me."

Grace bent closer. "I'm here. You're safe now." The woman reminded her of the widow Berkshire, her grandmother's old friend, but it had been years since Grace had last seen her.

Anger churned at the sight of blood on the elderly woman's brow, trickling into graying hair splayed unpinned on the hard-packed lane. Dirt and grit smeared her black dress.

Grace should have run down that fella.

Boot steps from behind shot her around.

"Let me help."

A cowboy moved in, hands in view, eyes steady. Clearly not the attacker, but unknown.

He knelt next to the woman, gently pressed his fingers against her wrist, and seemed to listen with his dark eyes. "Rapid, but that's to be expected. Did you see her fall?"

His voice matched his eyes. Confident and calm as deep water. Kind.

He sat back on his heels, and Grace let go a measure of tension.

"She didn't fall—someone hit her."

The cowboy stood and surveyed the area, settling on the river path.

"That's the way he ran." Grace pointed. "After I charged him on Harley here."

The stranger glanced at Harley, then Grace, and back to the injured woman. "She runs the boarding house—Mrs. Berkshire. Let's get her inside, or at least out of the dirt and up on the porch."

Grace sucked in a breath. She'd been right about the woman's identity.

A noise drew her attention to the feed store behind them, where a heavyset clerk clambered down the back steps.

"What on earth?"

"We need the doctor," she told him as he approached.

Mrs. Berkshire rubbed her forehead and flinched. "That boarder—he—he robbed me."

Grateful for the cowboy's assistance, Grace slid her hands beneath the widow's arms, expecting him to pick up her feet.

"I've got her." Unhesitating but not boorish, he scooped her up as if she weighed nothing and carried her through the rickety gate and up to a rocker on the boarding house porch. With a commanding glare, he told the clerk, "The lady asked you to get the doctor."

Already breathless from hurrying the short distance, red patches blotched the clerk's face, but he ran off toward Main Street.

Grace smoothed matted hair from Mrs. Berkshire's temple. An egg-sized lump rose above the abrasion. Again she leaned close, calming her voice. "Can you hear me?"

Thin eyelids fluttered open, eyes dulled with confusion.

"What—where am I—" Her breath quickened more than Grace thought natural.

She took the grasping hand, surprised by its strength. "You're on your front porch. You fell."

"He—he …" She struggled to push herself up, and Grace gently held her in place.

"That young man—he—" Suspicion narrowed her already drawn features. "Who are *you*?"

"I'm Grace Hutton, your friend Annie's granddaughter." She perched on her knees beside the rocker, one hand atop the widow's.

The cowboy's boots scraped behind her. "Your attacker was a boarder?"

At the question, Mrs. Berkshire blinked and looked toward the lane where the doctor came hurrying around the corner, bag in hand. The clerk followed several paces behind, wiping his brow.

"Mrs. Berkshire, I see you are out and about this morning." The doctor came up the steps and stopped before the rocker, observing her face with none of the jocularity that colored his voice.

She huffed and swatted as if he were a fly. "Oh, go on, Miller. I'm fine as frog hair."

"And twice as prickly." He opened his bag and pulled out a stethoscope. "Closer to porcupine hair, I'd say."

Grace swallowed her amazement.

The doctor leaned in. "You caught me out on my rounds. Perfect timing. Now I'm going to take a listen to that ticker of yours, so don't get all crotchety on me."

Again with the swat. "You'll do no such thing."

Unmoved by her resistance, he put the ear pieces in his ears and offered Grace the opposite end, nodding toward Mrs. Berkshire's chest. "Would you mind doing the honors, Miss, er, Miss—"

"Hutton. Grace Hutton."

His expression shifted to recognition. "I thought you looked familiar. What a welcome home this must be for you!"

Familiar with the device, she accepted the chest piece and placed it on the left side of the widow's bodice. "Rest easy, Mrs. Berkshire. I worked one of these during an emergency in Kansas City. I'll hold this end for the doctor while he listens to your heart."

Grace's smile was met with steely eyes and pursed lips.

Silence ticked by like a mantle clock, but Grace read no alarm on the doctor's face. He finally removed the ear tubes, rolled the stethoscope around itself, and dropped it into his bag.

"I'm afraid you'll be hanging around a while longer, Mrs. Berkshire. You have the heart of a horse."

Duly offended, the widow huffed again and pulled herself up. "Well, I never!"

"I'm certain of it, madam. Now if you will please sit still, I'll clean that nasty scrape on your head. Are you sure you were not tipping the brandy bottle a little early in the day?"

Grace nearly burst but held Mrs. Berkshire back from throttling the good doctor. No doubt, that was his intention with so belligerent a bed-side manner. Or porch-side, as the case might be. He certainly had a unique way of determining the stamina of his reluctant patient and would have been a boon to the cast and crew of Cody's traveling show.

After a quick but gentle prodding through matted hair and then dressing the wound, he took a small bottle from his satchel and handed it to Grace as he stood.

"If you will see that she takes two teaspoons three times a day for three days, I believe she will soon be fit as a fiddle."

Grace shot to her feet. "But I don't—"

"Not a problem. I'll send a bill along later." He took the widow's left arm and motioned for Grace to take the right. "Let's get Mrs. Berkshire settled into a comfortable chair inside before you administer the first dose."

Grace bit back an argument but lined it up right behind her teeth for quick retrieval in the parlor.

Was she supposed to drop everything and play nursemaid? Years of independence and the day's pressing business tested her Christian charity. Wasn't there anyone else to care for the widow Berkshire? What of the pastor? Or the Women's Charitable Society? Were they still around?

What would Grace's family think if she didn't come home tonight?

She snorted, most unladylike. Hard to imagine her brothers worrying over her whereabouts now that they had wives, but she at least owed their cook, Helen, an explanation.

A glance through the parlor's west window revealed Harley lipping sparse grass from the patchy yard. She could board him overnight at the livery, have him shod, and head back to the Rafter-H tomorrow. She'd come to town for that very reason anyway. And to look for a job.

But not this job.

Unprepared for Doc Miller's request, all Grace had with her was what she wore. Her split skirt, high-top boots, and show hat were hardly apparel for a nursemaid.

A telephone would certainly make things easier, but the Hutton brothers had no more strung a line out to the ranch than it had snowed there in July.

Shoving aside her disrupted plans, Grace bid the doctor good day and helped Mrs. Berkshire lift her feet to the settee. The woman had brightened considerably with the doctor's visit, but her temple was turning wicked shades of purple and black that spread into her eyebrow. She must be in pain.

Using a soup spoon from the kitchen for fear the woman wouldn't agree to two smaller doses, Grace administered the first round with a question. "Where do you keep your hair brush, Mrs. Berkshire? I can brush out the dirt and knots while you enjoy a cup of tea."

The widow screwed up her face like a petulant child. "It's Dorrie. I haven't been a *Mrs.* for twenty-five years, about as long as it's been since I took laudanum. Never forget the smell of it."

"But it will help with the pain, and I suspect you have a terrible headache." Grace held the spoon securely, not willing to risk her patient swatting it from her hand and splashing it all over the both of them.

"No thank you." Dorrie turned her head dramatically toward the window.

Grace could force her, but then she'd be as bad as the ruffian who had knocked her down.

"See that fine animal out by the fence? That's my horse, Harley. He's a bona fide Wild West show performer—Harley the

Wonder Horse. Right now I'm guessing the Wonder Horse is wondering where his next meal is coming from. I need to get him to the livery. But I can't do that until you take this medicine."

"Hmph. Put him in the back." A thin hand flicked over the widow's head, indicating the direction. "Barn, corral, everything including an overgrown pasture out there. And I won't charge you a thing."

"And I won't charge you for ministering to your needs."

Grace hadn't met her match yet, and Dorrie Berkshire sure wasn't going to earn the honor. "I am not moving until you take this."

Gray eyes slid a glance her way, observing the spoon held at mouth level. "You are as stubborn as your grandmother." She grabbed the spoon and shoved it in her mouth, then tossed it to the floor.

Grace picked up the spoon. "And as Grandmother Annie always said, temper tantrums aren't limited to young children."

Dorrie blushed, which merely provided a colorful backdrop for her deepening bruise.

"Where is your brush, if you don't mind my asking." Grace didn't care one bit if she minded and was prepared to go through every room of the house in order to find it. After all, she'd been here many times before.

"Upstairs. First door on the left."

Like a cobwebbed memory, the old house stirred a familiar sense of well-being, even the unusual way the stairs opened toward the kitchen. Grace hung her hat on the newel post and hurried up to the second floor.

Three doors opened from three sides of the hall, and she entered the one on the left. She found a hand mirror and hairbrush on the dresser, then gathered quilts and pillows from the bed and returned to the parlor. A pallet on the floor beside the settee would serve in case Dorrie rolled off while sleeping. At least she wouldn't break her neck.

And sleeping she was. Laudanum did that to a body.

Sudden realization stilled Grace's hands. What happened to the cowboy?

She looked through the window curtains fronting the porch, but he wasn't there. Nor was he in the lane that led to Main Street.

She shivered.

Where had he come from? At just the right moment, no less. And where had he gone?

Rubbing her arms, she went down the hall to the kitchen and found the back door locked. Relieved, she checked the front door, removed the key, and locked it from outside in case the ruffian who had caused this whole problem thought to return before she did.

~

Gathering Harley, Grace walked to the livery, her plans to find a job completely dashed. The town felt smaller than she remembered, despite some of the new storefronts she'd passed on her way in earlier that morning. Old favorites remained, like Reide's Bakery and the Ceylon Tea Store. The *Cañon City Record* held its own, as did the grocery, hardware, and paint stores. But she doubted any of those businesses would hire her.

Of course, the Denton Hotel and Raynold's Bank maintained their dignified status on Main Street. If Clara was still cooking at the Denton, maybe she'd take Grace on as a helper, though cooking wasn't exactly Grace's strong suit.

The Selig Polyscope studio was a new development. She'd heard about Cañon City flickers but had no opportunity to see one. Her traveling and performance schedule had left little down time as well as little skill to be used elsewhere. There weren't many calls for trick riding and fancy shooting.

As she approached the livery for the second time that morning, it seemed, well, *shorter.* Not as grand as it had been in her childhood, but as flat as the painted-tarp backdrops of buffalo herds and mountains stretched across arena floors.

In three and a half years, the atmosphere had changed.

She had changed.

Harley nuzzled her shoulder. At least she had him, thanks to Mr. Cody.

"Gracie, is that you?" An oak of a man in a smithy's leather apron gawked from inside the barn as if she was covered in war paint and feathers.

"As sure as that must be you, Smitty. Are you still in the farrier business?"

His black mustache stretched across his weathered face as he approached, and he offered his hand, then quickly jerked it back to his blackened apron.

Grace reached for his arm. "Give me that grimy hand. It's good to see you, Smitty."

He cast an approving eye on Harley. "Pretty fancy horse you've got there, Grace. Is he one of them gaited mountain horses I've heard about?" He walked around Harley like a bidder at an auction. "Odd color. Buckskin in reverse."

Grace had grown accustomed to people's comments. Harley's light mane and tail contrasted sharply with his dark chocolate coat. He'd been as sure on his feet as a Big Horn sheep until arthritis started creeping up on him. Maybe that's why Cody had let him go.

"You're looking at Harley the Wonder Horse. And you're right about his heritage. Though his ancestors hail from Kentucky, he's a full-blooded Rocky Mountain horse."

"Dangdest name I ever heard." Smitty leaned against Harley's front left shoulder and lifted his foot, smoothing a roughened hand over the worn shoe before letting the foot drop to the ground. "Seems like he ought to be an Appalachian horse."

"That's what some folks say. But he's actually come full circle for the breed. The original sire came from this high country."

She reached under Harley's neck and patted him on the off

side. "Can you have him shod by tomorrow morning?"

Smitty scratched his unshaved cheek. "Your rough-ridin' days over with the Wild West outfit, or you home for a visit? If ya' don't mind my askin'."

"I don't mind you asking." But she wasn't about to tell him. The whole town would know in a half hour. "And can you board him overnight?"

Smitty's mustache twitched again. "I'm backed up some on shoeing, but I'll move him to the head of the line. Anything for a Hutton."

Inwardly, she balked. "Thank you."

She stepped back with a casual air. "You wouldn't know of anyone around here looking for help, would you?"

Smitty took the reins. "I've heard you're quite the hand with a bronc."

Grace knew the jibes would come. Outside of the show ring, people didn't know what to make of her. But the twitch of the blacksmith's mustache confirmed his good-natured affection.

"Breaking horses to ride or pull a buggy," she said. "Something simple."

He nodded. "I'll put the word out."

She'd probably ruined her welcome with the feed store clerk, so she turned toward the main part of town. If she didn't dally, she'd have time to check at least one business before the widow woke up.

CHAPTER TWO

In the first block, a single word in fancy gold script on a storefront window caught her eye. She didn't remember what had been there before, but this morning it was clear: *Hats.*

In smaller, fancier script, *Dan Waite* curved beneath the larger word. Shielding daylight with one hand, she peered through the glass into the long, narrow store. Feeling all of twelve at such gawking, she reached for the doorknob.

No bell rang as she entered. Strange. Anyone could walk in off the street and make away with several toppers.

As she quietly closed the door, she tasted the tang of craftmanship. Beaver felt and leather, sulfur and machine oil. Part haberdashery, part harness shop. A typical tin ceiling stretched above it all with a wood floor beneath, like most establishments on Main Street.

Shelves lined one side of the store with various blocks and unfinished hat bodies. Tall, shapeless crowns rose above shorter, modest blanks. Wide brims and narrow.

The other side of the store offered finished merchandise in an array of colors from near white to well-deep black.

She touched the brim of her own hat, the grosgrain-bound edge rough beneath her fingertips. The hat had cost a hefty chunk of her salary, but it had been worth it to receive Mr. Cody's approving nod when he saw her in costume.

Toward the back, the hats thinned out and reels of ribbon, tanned hides, and satin cloth filled the shelves. A Singer sewing machine topped a long workbench with a chair before it. Curtains tempted her to push them aside, but she knew well the importance of not allowing the public behind the scenes. This was a workshop as well as a hattery. Possibly a home.

Apparently, no one was about, so she stepped behind the counter and ran her fingers over the smooth, unshaped brims waiting to be formed to a buyer's preference. Her own brim turned up in a gentle sweep on the sides with a green hat band setting off the creamy eggshell. Showy, with a flair for performing. Not a hat she'd wear gathering cows, but all she had at the moment.

No wonder Smitty had stared.

She liked what she saw—quality rather than mass production. Waite obviously knew what he was doing. His merchandise bore testimony of his hatter's expertise—his touch, his eye, and the ability to bring a felted hat body to life and crown the wearer with durability, style, or both. Bowlers sat beside cattlemen's toppers. No straws.

A smile pulled at the obvious exclusion.

"You lookin' for something in particular?"

~

Grace Hutton turned, and two dagger-sharp eyes pinned him to the floor, green as her hat band and as unusual as she was—out of place with her high, pinched crown and fancy boots. Like something from a Wild West show.

Like what he'd seen that morning at the boarding house.

Recognition eased her stance, and she relaxed, smoothing one hand down the side of her split skirt. "Oh. It's you."

Not sure what to make of her comment, he ran a fine-grade sand block over the flat brim of a form on the workbench.

"I mean, thank you for your help this morning," she said. "Mr. Waite."

"Dan."

Her gaze slid to the back of the shop. "I didn't see you there."

Nor had she heard him come around the curtain, watching

her evaluate his wares. "I'm glad I could help with Mrs. Berkshire. Good timing." God's timing was more like it. He never waited so late to walk outside in the morning and take in the fresh air.

Heat flushed her face as well as what he could see of her neck between her open collar and silk scarf.

"I was, um, looking for a hat."

He tipped his head toward the street. "Milliner's two doors down."

Her shoulders drew back and her chin came up. "I'm looking for a hat, not a bonnet."

As feisty a filly as he'd seen in town.

A smile pressed and he shut it down. "Is the hat for your husband?"

"No." Expressionless.

"Your father."

"No." Quieter.

"Your brother?"

"Ha!" She quickly covered her mouth and cleared her throat. "No, not my brothers." She held his eye.

He couldn't be sure with that wide brim, but he thought she cocked an eyebrow. The right one.

"Do you not serve female customers?"

"If I had any." He might be looking into the face of one at the moment. All business, no flirt about her. Which suited him fine.

She moved along the counter, one hand skimming the top. "How long have you been here? I don't remember a hatter."

"A while."

Danged if she didn't squint.

Reaching the bench, she laid her fingers in the path of his sanding.

It was almost more than he could tolerate, her interfering with his work. But her hands set him back—not rough, but not pampered either. Capable. Comfortable, he imagined. Unlike the steel he sensed in her spine.

Pretty, this woman with straw-colored hair and the gumption to chase off an attacker. She was neither young nor old, but a certain wisdom edged her eyes that said she'd seen places far from Cañon City.

Her finger bore no ring.

"I want a hat to replace the one I'm wearing. Darker and no ribbon." She glanced at the sewing machine. "Maybe a thin one."

He lifted his hand as if to take it from her head. "May I?"

She shied and removed it herself, then handed it to him.

Warmth filled the crown from her wearing of it, and the sweatband let go a subtle hint of soap. Something a woman would use. Something he'd not smelled in all his years making hats. 'Course, his customers had all been men.

"I'm curious, where'd you get this?"

"Denver."

Clever. As vague as he had been. He knew of at least three hatters in Denver, but he didn't recognize the work. "Wanna leave this with me to match the size?"

She took the hat. "I wear a seven."

Large for a woman, but that sandy hair more than likely took up an eighth of an inch. Maybe more if the thickness of her braid said anything.

"May I set it on a form?"

She handed it over, and he pulled a block from the shelf. Perfect seven.

"Give me two weeks, then come back in and I'll shape the brim to your liking."

He returned it to her, and she settled it lower in the front as if hiding her eyes. "You need a deposit?"

A cough from behind the curtains drew her attention and she raised her head, curiosity flickering in the green.

"A dollar."

She pulled a coin purse from her riding skirt and handed

him two fifty-cent pieces.

"All right, Grace Hutton."

"You remembered." Surprise softened her words until she remembered to be gritty. "I'll return in two weeks."

She crossed the room and paused at the door, speaking over her shoulder. "And thank you again. It was kind of you to help."

She turned the knob. "Do you know of any place in town where I could find work? Maybe someone who needs a horse trained?"

"Did you ask at the—"

"Yes, I did."

Alrighty then. "If I hear of anything, I'll let you know when you come for your hat. Or you could check back in a couple days." Not sure why he added that last part.

Outside, she looked both ways, then struck out across Main Street toward the lane to the river.

He watched her disappear behind the feed store, probably returning to the boarding house.

"Da—" A sharp cough broke off the end of his name.

"Coming."

Blast. He'd forgotten to ask what color she wanted. *Darker* could be anything from natural beaver to coal black.

But he'd not forget her name. *Grace.*

She moved with it.

CHAPTER THREE

Well, that was the last person Grace expected to run into this morning—the mysterious cowboy who had helped her with Dorrie. And what had she been thinking, going into a hatter's rather than someplace she might find work?

When she'd said the hat was for herself, he looked up at her as if she were stone-cold crazy. Maybe she was. Hugh thought so when she had decided to ride with Bill Cody.

Waite had wanted to laugh. She could see it crawling across his face and hiding somewhere behind his eyes.

But he was an uncommon man. Different from others in this fast-paced, changing world. Steady, it seemed. Purposeful, with a quiet quality about him.

She returned to the boarding house somewhat nudged off center by the way Dan Waite had held her hat. Brushed his fingertips over it like it was sacred. Looked at her as if he could see right through to all her past and brokenness.

He remembered her name.

She shivered—again. Twice in one day, and the weather hadn't even turned yet.

Overgrown day lilies crowded the boarding house like an Elizabethan collar on an old woman, and familiarity struggled with obvious neglect. Chipped paint and sagging shutters defied the house's architecture, not to mention her memories.

And then there was the feed store in front of it that still felt ill-placed. It used to be a church—her grandfather's church, or so Mama had said.

The barn wasn't much better off, but it might be a good idea to take Dorrie up on her offer. Harley came first now. He was in good hands with Smitty, but her savings wouldn't last indefinitely, and that hat she'd ordered wasn't going to be cheap.

Again her mind meandered to the hatter and his strong, confident bearing, so unlike the feedstore clerk and the scoundrel she'd chased off—a boarder, Dorrie had said.

Maybe Grace could be her next boarder. Her grandparents' house could be home to both herself and Harley, at least for a while.

Half the answer to her needs.

It could also be the Lord's provision.

All things work together for good to them that love God.

As a child, she'd memorized the words, encouraged by her mother who quoted Grandmother's insistence that memorization was the "quickest and shortest route to God's comfort and strength."

Apparently, *all things* included bad things too, and what could be worse than Dorrie's assault? Could anything good really come from that?

She quietly unlocked the front door and stepped inside. Dorrie was out cold on the parlor settee, but her still form worried Grace into bending for a kiss of breath against her cheek. Satisfied that the woman lived, she went to the kitchen in search of sustenance.

Two fresh loaves of bread had cooled to stone on the counter, and she covered one with a clean, damp cloth and an upside-down bowl—a secret she'd learned from Lilly Mae Murphy, trick-shot extraordinaire. From the other loaf, she sliced two pieces and set them on a plate. A butter dish and tarnished sugar bowl shared the center of the kitchen table, and a camp-sized graniteware pot offered tepid coffee.

She stoked the cook-stove fire, moved the pot to the front burner, and sat down with the bread and a butter knife.

A gas light hung above the table, reminiscent of pre-electric days. The ranch didn't have electric lights either, one of the common conveniences Grace had enjoyed in her travels. Not with the show itself, but hotels, dining establishments, and gala-hosting homes all boasted the latest innovations. Telephones even. This house still carried the touch of her grandparents.

A vague memory snagged on the edge of her heart and cleared into focus. She'd almost forgotten.

Stepping quietly along the hall and past the rising stairs, she stopped where they reached the second floor. Before her, the paneled wall gave no hint of what lay behind it, and she ran her fingers along vertical planes until one gave beneath pressure.

Directly across from the parlor, she glanced over her shoulder at the widow, then pressed again. The panel clicked. Her heart leaped.

She'd been in this hidden room a few times as a child, but what she remembered most clearly was the smell.

Books.

A thrill chased up the back of her neck as she slid the panel aside, revealing a long but shallow room that now smelled of dust and neglect. But beneath that stirring layer hid the original scents: leather, paper, ink.

More spacious than a private room on a train, but not by much, one step took her forward into her family's past.

A narrow sash window on the east wall would welcome the morning if its shade was pulled. She gave it a tug and it snapped to its roller, sending a dust cloud into the room. But even the indirect afternoon light opened the dismal space, revealing the floral pattern of the rug beneath her feet and the wainscoting on the walls.

A large cherrywood desk anchored one end of the room, backed by floor-to-ceiling shelves filled with books. Treasures, she considered them, and she longed to journey through their pages and run her fingers over the covers. A lower shelf held books on veterinary medicine, but most housed volumes on religious subjects with a few novels tucked in at the ends of the rows.

A black Bible laid atop the desk, drawing Grace to mine its riches. She moved around to the other side and opened its cover—

Presented to Rev. Caleb Hutton ~ St. Joseph, Missouri ~ 1859

Below his name, *Married Annie Whitaker, December 29, 1860, Cañon City, Jefferson Territory* followed by two births:

Whitaker Hutton, born October 15, 1861, Cañon City, Colorado Territory

Martha Mae Hutton, born February 20, 1867, Cañon City, Colorado Territory

Grace ran her finger over her papa's name—he'd gone by Whit, named after his Grandpa Whitaker. She'd always thought she'd like to continue the name through her own children. But one should have a husband first, before children, and that detail had escaped her.

Pushing away the sense of lack, she held the book upright on its spine, letting it open naturally to the most often-read passages. The first was the book of Jeremiah, and she quietly read the underlined passage, knowing beforehand what it would say.

"For I know the thoughts that I think toward you, saith the Lord, thoughts of peace and not of evil, to give you an expected end."

A familiar promise, but it sank deeper into her spirit, reading it from her grandfather's Bible. Had it carried special meaning for him?

She smoothed her hand over the page as if it connected with her heritage and glanced at the opposite end of the room. A low day-bed angled away from one corner where a small table and oil lamp offered light for one who wanted to rest and read. Perfect for Dorrie this evening. Much more comfortable than the settee, and no doubt safer than climbing the stairs.

Grace suddenly envied the one who would lie here tonight in the lap of her legacy.

Before leaving, she lifted the sash window and left the sliding door open, encouraging fresh air to wash the room.

"You're burning the coffee."

Across the narrow hallway, Dorrie sat upright on the settee, knitting needles clacking away like the wheels on a distant train.

"Oh!" Grace ran to the kitchen where coffee was boiling onto the burner and hissing into oblivion.

"It's not ruined." Dorrie's voice carried clearly from the parlor with no hint of injury or discomfort.

She must be a tough old thing.

Guilt wormed into Grace at branding the woman so unkindly. The same thing would probably be said of her one day.

"Just add water and let it cook a little more."

Dorrie sounded as if she too had traveled cross-country living on the rails, and Grace imagined she could have held her own in Cody's camp.

She buttered the bread slices she'd abandoned for exploration and set one on another saucer. A tea tin changed her mind about salvaging the coffee, so she filled a copper kettle with water and set it to boil.

While the water heated, she discovered a small screened-in room that took up half the back porch and had a separate entrance. A new addition since she'd been there, and a nice place to sleep in warm weather. Quite another matter in winter.

A narrow cot, a nightstand, and a braided rag rug gave it a bit of a welcoming air, though the ticking and blanket looked as if someone had left in a hurry.

Could it have been the boarder Dorrie accused of robbing and attacking her?

The kettle whistled its readiness.

Grace located a strainer for the tea, prepared two cups, and took them to the parlor.

"If you look in the larder, I'm sure you'll find a jar of elderberry jam." The needles clacked on, never missing a beat.

She found the jam, spread it generously on both slices of bread, and returned to the parlor where Dorrie laid her needles aside and took the saucer with an affirmative nod.

"You've grown up quite a bit since I saw you last, Grace dear."

Evidently her mind had cleared from the morning's dramatic incident, or the trauma had jogged her memory.

"Yes, ma'am." Grace took an old burgundy chair sitting at a right angle to the settee. The elderberry jam was, well, heavenly, evoking images of summer, and tree swings, and creek water splashing against her bare legs.

Over the teacup, Dorrie scrutinized her, head to toe and back again. "As a grown woman, you are the very image of your father's mother, Annie."

Grace considered the remark a blessing. She set her bread plate down and looked more closely at the little woman who had brushed her own matted hair and twisted it into a knot at her neck.

"Thank you. I consider that an honor."

Dorrie's wrinkles deepened into a warm smile. "She passed not long after you left to ride in Cody's traveling show, and I must tell you, she was proud of your pluck, as she put it."

Grace regretted not returning for the service, but she had received word too late.

"As you know, she was older than I by several years, but we became quite close and I moved in here with her."

Grace knew that as well, but who better to tell the story than the one who lived it?

"She wanted her home to be available to those who needed a place to stay, and together we opened it for meals and rented rooms."

Dusty images stirred in Grace's memory—a snowy graveside service for her grandfather years before. Grandmother's mention of a boarding house, though at the time Grace didn't know what that meant.

Dorrie paused a moment before addressing her again, an added depth of tone in her voice. "I see her fearlessness in you. The only thing different is your hair. You have more than your share, as did your grandmother, but hers was fiery red to match her spirit."

Grace's eyes welled, spilling first across her soul with the healing of home she'd not found when she returned to the ranch three weeks ago. Her brothers and their wives had welcomed her. So had Helen and the boys. But she didn't fit there. Just like she hadn't fit before she left with the Wild West Show.

But here? In her grandmother's home with a woman who had known her so well?

Grace pressed her arm against her eyes, determined not to be a blithering twit. "I heard often of her remarkable romance with my grandfather, Caleb. I wanted a love like that of my own."

Surprised by her unplanned admission, she hoped she hadn't misjudged the widow. No one alive on this earth knew her secret.

Dorrie closed her eyes and sipped her tea, then looked at Grace from a place familiar yet not. "Perhaps the reason you left when you did?"

Grace blinked and more tears advanced. Such painful cleansing in truth's wake. "Yes," she whispered.

Dorrie laid a hand on Grace's knee. "And did you find it?"

Rushing in on that simple question came the vision of what Grace thought she had found—Captain Jackson Gayer, fine and formal in his cavalry uniform, sword at his side.

She shook her head, and her throat squeezed off all sound but the deep fissure of the final reality—Jackson in the arms of another woman. The beautiful Lakota princess, White Feather, no less.

"Looking back, I doubt that a two-timing, imitation cavalry cheat was what the Lord had in mind for me. I went that route all on my own, ignoring the early warnings."

Again, the widow's hand, patting her knee, then withdrawing. "Many are the hearts that have suffered the same affliction. But as you must have already suspected, the Lord has something much better in store."

Grace wrapped her arms around her middle to keep from falling apart. "Do you really think so?"

"Ah, child. You are under the great covering grace of God. He sees you, and He knows what You need better than you do."

Dorrie pushed to her feet and Grace quickly joined her, unwilling to let the slight woman fall.

"Come with me, dear. I've something to show you."

They crossed the hall and entered the study, where Dorrie pulled a large scrapbook from a lower shelf and opened it on the desk.

As if wiping the years away, she brushed her aged hand across an image of three couples, each standing arm in arm and smiling more than Grace had seen in most photographs.

Dorrie pointed to the couple in the center. "That is your grandmother and grandfather, Annie and Caleb Hutton, on their wedding day."

Grace had never seen the tintype and she clutched at her scarf, surprised to look back through time at her origins, yet somehow comforted in what she saw in the dusty hues. Happiness and hope were evident in the faces. Especially one face in particular. One in the center.

Her own.

~

Dan's father nested against pillows on the narrow, spindle bed. Quilts and blankets hid everything but his head and an empty glass tilted in his veined hand.

"You didn't ask her what color." A lesser cough.

His breathing was as shallow as a babe's, but Daniel Waite, Sr. could hear a satin ribbon hit the floor.

"Give me your glass and I'll fill the pitcher too. You warm enough?"

"Yes." Pop sank deeper into the pillow, as thin and faded as the pale fabric. Skin clung to the bones of his skull and shrank into hollows beneath his cheek bones. His condition was killing him—killing him before the hot springs and mineral water they'd come for could heal him.

Dan set the pitcher of iron water on the nightstand and held the glass to his father's lips. "It's tepid, the way you like."

Fragile hands that once blocked beaver-felt crowns and stitched leather sweat bands trembled in weakness as they took the glass. "I can hold it."

Yes, Pop could still hold his own glass, but for how long? A minute? Ten seconds, before it slid through his fingers?

Dan stooped over him, willing strength into the dying man's grasp as if fisting his own hands and gritting his teeth would make it so.

Doctors had told him Pop suffered from "nervous heart disease, " a condition brought on by sudden trauma or loss. The name didn't fit the malady. Pop wasn't nervous and his chest didn't hurt, but it was a fact that the death of Dan's mother five years before had been the start of his father's decline.

The glass slipped, and Dan caught it before it hit the quilt. "I'll close up early and we'll go to the Hot Springs Hotel."

Pop sucked in a breath. "You'll never make any money if you keep your door closed all hours of the day." Another cough, and he slid farther beneath the blankets and closed his eyes.

Leaving him to rest, Dan finished a previous Derby order, began another, and had only one customer before locking the door, turning the sign to "closed," and letting his father know.

"I'm going for the buggy. Do you need anything before I leave?"

Pop shook his head, eyes closed. The sandwich Dan had made earlier lay uneaten in a saucer on the night stand. If grief didn't rob the elder Waite of life and breath, starvation would.

Dan went out the back, locking the door. This was a fine setup for his sick father—living in the back of a store on Main

Street. Dan refused to take a room and leave him all day in a hotel with no one to look in on him. He'd given Berkshire's boarding house some thought, but after this morning's incident, that option was off the table.

Good God, what am I supposed to do?

Smitty got the mare and buggy up in no time, and Dan drove around to the back of the shop. No wind or breeze to speak of, but he still bundled his father in blankets and a stocking cap as if it were snowing, and carried him to the waiting buggy.

His heart bore a much heavier load than his arms as he lifted Pop to the seat. After securing blankets around his father's ankles and adjusting the muffler at his neck, Dan propped a pillow between the arm rest and the man. The dearest, smartest, strongest man he'd ever known, now with less stamina than a child.

Since his wife's death, Daniel Waite, Sr. had all but given up.

Dan had moved back into his parents' Denver home, worked to salvage the hat shop and restore his father's desire to live. He'd failed at both.

His last hope was Cañon City and the Hot Springs Hotel and bath house. Healing waters, he'd read. Good for all sorts of ailments and diseases. They'd come last year, and Dan bought the long, narrow shop, with living quarters above that they couldn't use because of the stairs. At least there was a storeroom.

He flicked the reins, and the mare moved down the alley at an easy pace, turned at the juncture of 7th street, and then west onto Main at the Denton Hotel.

Traffic was light for a Thursday, and for that, Dan was grateful. Fewer automobiles and less noise made the three-mile drive out of town to the hot springs almost pleasant. Gold-flecked cottonwoods lined the Arkansas River on both banks, harbingers of fall. Occasional pastures supported small dairies or farms. Fruit trees and gardens bore witness to the area's early culture as a bread basket for mining camps, but farther from town, granite outcroppings and scattered juniper announced the canyon mouth of the Royal Gorge. A land of great contrast.

He snapped the reins against the lagging mare, and as they approached the hotel, it was clear that it had once been a grand lady. The faded lawns must have been lush and green, yet now they seemed foreboding, predictive of the man he was trying to save. A skeletal footbridge spanned the river to a former train stop, it too a shadowy remnant. Even the river itself whispered by, its waters low and tired this late in the season.

When Dan stopped near the entrance, he turned his back on the dreary setting and lifted his father from the buggy. A few wheeled chairs waited nearby to make the trek easier.

Fifty cents bought a bath in the thermal waters, and the steam greeted them in their private room. Dan hoped a good, hot soaking would sooth Pop's aches and help restore his withering muscles.

But he couldn't risk succumbing to the water himself, for he needed every ounce of muscular response and a clear head for his father's safety. The humidity and warmth once proved a personal danger when Pop had nearly slipped beneath the surface.

It would not happen again.

CHAPTER FOUR

That evening after a supper of more toast and jam, Grace brought coffee to the parlor and opened the front door to draft a breeze. She couldn't leave Dorrie tonight, but she *must* return to the ranch tomorrow morning. That would give her time to get back to Cañon City with the buckboard, her trunk in the back, and Harley tied to the tail gate. Hugh or Cale could pick it up their next trip to town.

But she still needed someone to stay with Dorrie tomorrow morning until she returned.

On the settee, Dorrie sipped and nodded approval of the coffee. "Perfect. And you can't sleep on the porch."

Grace had anticipated the discussion and glanced at her charge. "Why don't you sleep out there. You'd have a cool breeze."

"Not on your life." She downed the rest of her coffee, hot as it was. "The porch is where Oglethorpe slept and I haven't had a chance to wash his linens. I won't be sleeping on his lice and bed bugs."

Grace shuddered in spite of the warm evening. "I'll do that for you and then beat the ticking."

Dorrie lifted her chin in offense. "I am not an invalid. I can do my own laundry."

In spite of their connection over her grandmother, Grace would not relinquish the upper hand. "Not on my watch, and I'll be here until Doc Miller tells me otherwise." She held the woman's eye. "It will be a waste of your time to argue."

"Hmph."

Dorrie should sleep downstairs, at least tonight, but it was too late for laundry this evening. And even as petite as she was, the settee was too small for anything but a nap.

"I take it Oglethorpe is the long-haired man who attacked you."

Dorrie stiffened and a muscle in her jaw flexed. "And robbed me."

"What did he take?"

"The money he'd paid me for a week's room and board. He found where I'd put it temporarily—in the soda tin on the kitchen window sill."

She pulled a hankie from her long sleeve and pressed it smooth on her lap. "Thankfully, I don't keep it all there."

"I'll tell the sheriff and take care of the bedding. In the meantime, we have to get you settled for the evening. What about the study?"

A cutting side glance. "You think I can't make it up the stairs, don't you."

It wasn't a question. And Grace didn't need an enemy. She needed cooperation if she was to care for this hard-headed woman she was beginning to think of in grandmotherly terms.

She finally bribed Dorrie into sleeping in the study, promising no more laudanum if she cooperated. Blankets from the floor pallet next to the settee worked perfectly on the daybed, and Grace used the remaining quilts to cover the ticking on the back porch after beating it as an effigy of a certain cavalry captain. Satisfaction increased with each swing of the carpet beater she'd found in the pantry.

When Doc Miller stopped by unexpectedly before Dorrie retired, Grace served chamomile tea.

"I do believe you are in good hands, Mrs. Berkshire," he said. "It's best that you not go up and down the stairs for at least a week. Give yourself a chance to get over the trauma and let Miss Hutton run your errands as well. Just rest."

He exchanged a dialogue-laden look with Grace.

"Hmph." Dorrie brushed invisible lint from her lap.

Apparently satisfied, the doctor downed his tea. "How long can you stay, Miss Hutton?"

"Grace, please." She was short on formalities but long on efficiency. It didn't hurt that staying at the boarding house made it easier to find work in town. "As long as necessary."

"Excellent." He set his tea cup and saucer on a nearby end table and picked up his satchel. "Well then, I'll be on my way. You know where my office is if you have any questions, but I'll be by again on Monday."

He stood and adjusted his spectacles. "Good evening, ladies. I'll see myself out."

Before the door clicked behind him, Dorrie mumbled, "You bet your bifocals you will."

"What have you got against Doc Miller?" Grace said, muffling a chuckle.

"He called me old."

"He did not. I was sitting right here the entire time."

Dorrie pursed her lips and hiked her chin up again. "He most certainly did. Last fall when I broke my finger nailing up shutters on the screen porch."

Dorrie Berkshire had more spit and vinegar than many a man, let alone elderly women.

"And how did you do that?"

"With a hammer." Absently, she rubbed her left index finger. "Wish I'd had it in hand when Oglethorpe pulled his prank."

~

The next morning Grace snuggled beneath heavy quilts on the cot, waking slowly to cool, clean air sifting through the porch screens. No trace of soot, coal, or dirty straw. And not stifling or stuffy. She could get used to this arrangement, at least until snow flew—

Her nose flared. Was that coffee she smelled?

Her blouse not long enough for decency, she tugged off the top quilt and swathed herself with it. One turn of the cold doorknob took her to the open porch, and another let her inside the kitchen and its aromatic swirl of ham and fried potatoes.

Dorrie flipped over something in the skillet and turned to face her. "About time. I was afraid you'd died out there." A short huff and the bounce of narrow shoulders betrayed ill-disguised humor.

"What are you doing up? I thought you'd sleep in at least until after sunup with that goose egg on your head."

Dorrie poured a cup of coffee from the pot that was nearly as big as herself and set it on the table. "This is a boarding house, you know. I can't have my boarders missing out on their morning cup." She indicated the cream and sugar in the center of the table next to the elderberry jam and a plate of sliced bread. "Help yourself."

Snugging the quilt tighter, Grace took a chair and did just that.

"What do you charge for room and board?"

The widow set a plate before her, followed by a full place setting of dinnerware and a napkin. "Depends. Male or female?"

"Female. I happen to be in the market for work and a room in town." The first bite of ham and potatoes was as good as it smelled.

Dorrie joined her at the table with a saucer and cup. Coffee in the cup, breakfast on the edge. "I could use a little help with cleaning and such, I suppose. Not that I'm in need, mind you." She forked a potato slice, opened her mouth, and grimaced.

"Does it hurt to chew?" Grace leaned in and eyed the bruise that had blackened considerably.

Dipping her head as if hiding an important truth, Dorrie dabbed her mouth with a napkin, distorting what she mumbled before stating clearly, "I see you slept on the porch last night despite my objection."

A smile slipped into Grace's voice. "It was wonderful. After I beat the ticking, of course. But the fresh air was exactly what I needed."

"You won't be staying there come late fall, even with the shutters on. You'll want to move upstairs."

Late fall was more than two months away, surely enough time to find work and another place to stay.

A note of sadness slipped in behind that last thought. "I'm quite familiar with autumn in the Rockies. One can waken to a golden Indian summer or a foot of snow."

Dorrie laughed—the first sign of mirth Grace had seen in the brief time she'd spent with the woman.

Grace wasn't keen on keeping house, but if it put a roof over her head, she was willing to help. And from the amount of food Dorrie had on her saucer, dishwashing would be minimal.

"Is that how you eat all the time? You don't have enough there to keep a bird alive."

"Well, that's good, isn't it, since I'm not a bird." Dorrie winced in a few more bites, set her coffee aside, and took her plate to the sink. "You'll have to use hot water from the stove reservoir for the dishes. And there's a bathing room outside, built on to the privy with a wood stove and all. Nice and snug in the winter if I do say so. Go get dressed and I'll start the dishes this time."

This time?

With no desire to be compared to a trout, Grace consciously closed her gaping mouth at the rapid relegation to kitchen duty. Evidently, she was now an official boarder.

"Harley's at the livery. I'm going over to get him, then ride out to the ranch and let them know what I'm doing. I'll return around noon. Promise me you won't go upstairs."

Dorrie's chin hitched up, but it must have tugged something that hurt, and she lowered it with a wince.

Grace couldn't leave her alone, but who was going to stay

with her?

"Does the church still have a Women's Charitable Society?"

The widow's eyes narrowed to slits. "I do *not* want that bunch of old biddies in this house. As I said, I am not an invalid, and I most certainly do not want anyone's charity!"

If the situation hadn't been so dire, Grace would have laughed. But she didn't want to come back and find Dorrie lying at the bottom of the stairs.

"Promise me you won't go upstairs, wash Oglethorpe's bedding, or clean stalls in the barn." Her ploy worked and a near chuckle worked its way out of the widow's throat and bulged into her cheeks.

Grace didn't trust her. She was becoming quite fond of the feisty little woman, but she didn't trust her one bit.

~

As Grace approached the livery, Harley stood at the hitchrail and lifted his head with a familiar greeting. The man stroking his neck looked her way as well.

The hatter. With his own black hat.

"I see you've met Harley." She offered a smile to prove she wouldn't hold the caressing against him, then turned her back as she leaned into Harley's left shoulder and picked up his foot.

"Interesting color."

Everybody who saw him said that.

Smitty did nice work, but Grace checked all around just to be sure, ending up on the off side with the rail between herself and Mr. Waite.

"Would he be one of those Rocky Mountain horses?"

Sincerely surprised, she eyed Dan Waite with greater consideration. Few people knew what this breed was called. "Yes, he is. Are you familiar with them?"

The tiniest lift at the corner of his mouth suggested a smile. "My father grew up in Kentucky. He told me about them."

Waite pulled his fingers through Harley's mane. "Not quite flaxen, but close. Be a good color for a hat. Speaking of which—"

"Mr. Waite," Smitty interrupted, "your buggy's ready 'round back."

The hatter gave Harley a final pat and nodded at Grace. Then he paid the liveryman and disappeared inside.

Why would a cowboy like Dan Waite be renting a buggy? Didn't he have a horse of his own?

Maybe he has a sweetheart of his own.

An inexplicable drop in her mood fell further when Smitty told her the cost of shoeing. An entire dollar? She hadn't expected such a price in Cañon City, though she'd paid as much as four back East. She handed over the last silver dollar in her coin purse plus a dollar bill and change for board.

Too bad she couldn't set the widow up over here and have Smitty keep an eye on her.

At the absurdity of the thought, an idea ricocheted across her mind. Smitty wasn't the only neighbor around.

CHAPTER FIVE

Dan dropped the buggy weight in the alley behind the shop, climbed down, and unlocked the door. Soft snoring came from the windowless storeroom, and he paused, taking in his father's sunken form. Pop slept better in the mornings than he did at night, a phenomenon Dan couldn't figure out. Unless it had to do with a sense of escape. Escape from daylight and sorrow.

At night, Pop merely lay awake staring at the ceiling, tears collecting on his pillow.

"Morning, Pop."

His father snored on. Just as well. He'd run down to the café and get a cup of hot coffee.

For whatever reason, Grace Hutton's image materialized in his mind as he grabbed a mug off the sideboard, her thick braid hanging over her shoulder beneath her unusual hat. She'd said it was made in Denver, but no hatter's mark showed on the sweat band. He'd wager it was a showman's hat, and at that size, she might have gotten it off some fella working one of those Wild West Shows.

She'd stroked that Rocky Mountain horse with affection. Had she been in the shows herself? What was she—a crack shot like Phoebe Ann Mosey? Could Grace Hutton shoot the eye out of a double eagle at thirty paces?

Pounding yanked him to the back door and someone's frantic, "Hello!"

Determined to cuff whoever was making enough racket to wake the dead, he jerked the door open.

"What in blazes do you think you're—"

Grace Hutton herself took a step back, but only one. "I didn't know if you'd hear me and I have to talk to you. It's urgent."

Clenching his fists to keep from choking her, he stepped outside and pulled the door nearly shut. "Did you not see the sign in my window? I'm closed. It can wait until tomorrow." He glanced over his shoulder.

"I'm sorry to bother you, but I have an emergency situation and you were the first person who came to mind."

At her confession—or acting job—he crossed his arms. "You must be joking."

She braced her feet as if balancing for a steady shot. "The widow Berkshire needs your help again. The doctor assigned me to her care, but I have to let my family know, and there is no one to watch her while I'm gone."

This was the best tale he'd heard since moving to Cañon City. He glanced through the door again before looking her squarely in the eye. "Why are you telling me? Go get the doctor."

She hesitated, as if she hadn't thought of that herself, but quickly rallied.

"We're wasting time. I got her to promise she wouldn't try to climb the stairs, but that doesn't mean she won't. And I don't want to come back and find her out cold from a fall—or worse."

"Why didn't you mention this earlier at the livery?"

Her gaze wavered, but only a moment, then her hands clamped onto her waist. "I need someone to watch Mrs. Berkshire while I ride home and tell my family that I'll be staying in town for a few days. It will take a while to get there and back, and I don't want to leave her alone that long. You know her story—you were there. Can't you please come and sit with her? Or have you never cared for the infirm? Anyone other than yourself."

His teeth clenched, and his grip tightened on the door. He'd never lit into a woman and he wasn't about to start now. But she was worrying her luck and his patience.

"As you pointed out, you're closed."

He glanced again through the crack. Pop hadn't moved. What if it was *him* needing someone to be nearby?

Grace Hutton pressed her case. "You were so kind to help her yesterday, Mr. Waite. You know she lives *alone* at the boarding house. She rested well last night and is getting around, but I don't trust her not to dash up the stairs and roll all the way back down."

She paused, and he fully expected her to fall back on feminine appeal, pushing tears into the argument. She did not.

"I promise, I'll be back as close to noon as possible."

He ran a hand through his hair, resenting what he was thinking.

~

With a hop, Grace Hutton caught the stirrup with her left foot and landed in the saddle, then turned her Rocky Mountain horse away. Dan eased the door closed, her grateful eyes riveted in his brain and a house key pressed into his palm. He didn't need this. Not now. Not ever.

Neither did his father, and he hated to wake him. But he couldn't very well leave him wondering what happened to his son. Today's bath would have to wait, but as Dan approached the bed, peace rested on his father's face. As if he'd let go of the pain.

Startled by the possibility, Dan bent low over the shrunken body, relieved to feel a feeble breath. At least his father hadn't left for the great beyond.

With his hand gently resting on a bony shoulder, Dan straightened. "I'm leaving for a while, Pop. I won't be far, but I'll be gone a few hours. Will you be all right?"

Eyelids fluttered and his father's head turned. "I'm fine. Go on." A raspy breath. "Do something for yourself for a change."

Dan gently squeezed Pop's shoulder, hating the mantra that had become as common as daily bread. *Do something for yourself.*

That wasn't at all what he was doing.

Before leaving, he filled the glass on his father's night stand with water from the mineral springs, then opened a tin of crackers in case he got hungry and left them there too. It was about the only thing Pop ate anymore. Crackers and water, as if he were a prisoner.

In a sense, his father *was* a prisoner—of time, bad health, and a broken heart.

Dan locked the back door and took the buggy to the widow's. He'd return it when Grace Hutton got back.

As lovely a burr as he'd ever been snagged on, she badgered his thoughts. He knew of the Hutton brothers and their ranch north of Cañon City, but he hadn't known about a sister.

Evidently, Miss Hutton did things her own way and not theirs. And evidently, she'd been gone for a while. Why else would she ask *him* to help her and not a woman friend in town?

He drove around to an old barn hunched behind the boarding house, unhitched the mare, and led it into the empty corral. Better than leaving it standing on hard ground until Lord knew when.

The barn offered no feed or hay, but a hand pump provided water for the trough. Muddy and sparse, it coughed into the dry, wooden box. He let it run until it ran clear.

Miss Hutton had told him the key opened the front door, so he skirted around to the front porch, which was as far as he'd gone yesterday. Wiping his feet on a rug at the door, he turned the key and stepped into the aroma of fried potatoes and rose oil. Not the stuffy, old-house smell he'd expected.

The parlor opened to his right, and Mrs. Berkshire was curled like a cat on the settee. She looked a lot better than she had yesterday, and he figured her to be about the age of his father. A purple bruise colored her left temple, courtesy of the goose egg on that side of her head. He'd like to catch the no-account who did that.

~

Grace reined in at the sheriff's office, grateful that she could ground-tie Harley. Hitch rails were becoming few and far between.

The deputy there took down a description of Oglethorpe, the time of the robbery, and what he'd stolen, then promised to keep an eye peeled.

Nothing more could be done, and Grace felt the widow had seen the last of her money. She worried that Oglethorpe might return and told the deputy as much. Hence his peeled eye. A lot of good that would do.

She rode out of town and around the bend at the Soda Springs, heeling Harley into an easy lope. If she kept a steady pace with occasional walking, she'd make good time. But she wouldn't push Harley. No one was worth breaking him down. And besides, the hatter was with the widow. Hopefully she wouldn't chase him off.

Grace drew in a deep breath of clean Colorado air, along with sudden concern. Why did she trust the man so?

Yes, he set her a little off balance, but she had seen his tenderness yesterday with Dorrie. Sincerity in his eyes. A willingness to help. Was she crazy to give him access to the house?

Fear and doubt took hold and began climbing up the back of her throat. *Oh, Lord, am I so selfish that I would endanger Dorrie for my own welfare?*

Grace had been hoodwinked a time or two in her travels and learned the hard way that there was a con man around every corner.

But Dan Waite didn't strike her that way. She sensed there was more to him than a strong jaw and clear eyes as dark as her horse's coat.

Smitty hadn't given her pause over him either, and he knew everybody.

The clawing in her throat eased a bit.

Dan Waite had somebody on his mind, though. It was obvious by the way he kept looking back through the door this morning. She probably shouldn't have said what she did, but he hadn't argued that point when she begged for his help.

Yes, begged. Nothing to be proud of, but there it was.

Ochre bluffs cut against blue sky as she rode through a narrow canyon. Such rugged beauty had long ago rooted her love for Colorado. Always a contrast, much like herself. Dark pine and yellow aspen, snow-cold river and steaming hot springs. A heart crammed with wanderlust and a longing for home.

She slowed Harley to a walk, wondering if stark contrast had lured the hatter to Cañon City. Had he brought an ill loved one to take the waters at the springs, or did he merely scratch out a living crowning ranchers and merchants with his custom work?

What a puzzle he was, seemingly honest yet hiding something that was not one lick of her business.

Perhaps he had a sick wife.

The thought shuddered through her with enough vigor to send Harley into a lope.

She eased him back to a walk, setting her mind to more justifiable topics like Dorrie's attacker. What a cur, fiendish enough to strike an older woman. Grace would like nothing more than to see him running across an arena, dodging the sting of Lariat Leo's twin bullwhips.

A sneer pulled her dusty lips. She wouldn't mind taking a shot at him herself, though that would land her in jail now rather than the entertainment headlines of a newspaper.

From brave to brazen in less than three weeks. What was she going to do?

At twenty-four, she wasn't exactly every man's dream girl, and she quaked at the thought of ending up a ranch cook like Helen. The woman had certainly been a godsend for the family, but Grace would rather break horses and trail cows than cook all day for a bunch of ranchers.

"Lord, will I ever fit anywhere? Am I supposed to fit in?"

Harley's ears swiveled at the sound of her voice and he bobbed his head empathetically.

"You're right, old man." She leaned forward and rubbed his neck, tugging the reins a bit so he wouldn't take it as a sign to run. "We're an odd pair. Two of a kind, unlike everyone else and no slot to fill."

It wasn't being different that bothered Grace. It was being a burden, not able to pay her own way. Hers were not the skills of a homemaker. Maybe spending time with Dorrie Berkshire was exactly what she needed.

Two hours later, Harley ambled into the yard where Kip was swinging in the cottonwood tree. Her youngest nephew reminded her of herself—more pluck than good sense and always left out of the fun his two older brothers concocted as often as Helen made hot coffee.

"Where've you been?" Kip dragged his feet to stop the swing and ran her way.

Grace stepped down and caught him in her arms. "Hey there, cowboy. Who showed you that jump-hug trick."

He squeezed her neck, then slid to the ground. "You did, Aunt Grace."

The boy could smile the sun right out of the sky.

She looped Harley's reins on a corral pole. "Did you get left behind again?"

His head shot up and he stiffened. "No."

The set of his jaw said otherwise, but she knew well how resentment and jealousy colored a person's mind.

"How would you like to help me hitch up the mare and load my trunk in the buckboard?"

Kip's old-for-seven face screwed up in a question. "You're not leavin' us again, are you?"

"No, sir. I'll be close by, in town. I'm needed there to look after a sick lady."

She hadn't thought of it like that until this very minute. She was needed.

"Don't they have a doctor to do that?"

She squatted down to Kip's eye-level. "Yes, they do, but he has a lot of people he has to take care of, so he can't stay in one place for very long."

She straightened and gripped his shoulder. "If you help me, I'll show you how to throw a butterfly loop with your rope. And maybe how to catch your brothers' feet when they're walking, but you have to promise you won't tell on me or do it when your pa's watching."

A wicked scheme, she knew from experience, but the glee on Kip's face was worth all the switchings she'd taken as a girl. Hopefully, Kip's fate wouldn't be the same. Maybe she should stick to the butterfly.

"Tie Barlowe out on the hitch rail and brush her, and I'll be back to help you hitch her up. Deal?"

Her nephew's dark eyes sobered. He held out his hand for a shake, revealing the man that waited inside his little-boy body. "Deal."

On her way to the house, Grace calculated what she'd need and decided she'd take it all. She didn't have much anymore, and the steamer trunk she'd traveled with held everything. Few of her belongings remained at the ranch. Her room had housed the boys before her recent return, and the nursery harbored an old doll or two. Cale and Ella's little girl might enjoy playing with them in a year or so.

Helen wasn't in the kitchen, so Grace went back to the boys' bedroom, where she'd left her blue wardrobe trunk standing open. Its brass corner guards were tarnished from the miles, its latches and locks the same. But she cherished it—a gift from Lilly May Murphey when the sharp-shooter left the show.

"It'll get you where you're going, honey," Lilly had said, sentimentality tainting her tone. "And it'll protect your things if'n it gets tossed off the train. Which it did for me a time or two."

Grace knelt before the double-sided trunk, running her hands over a silk shirt that hung on a wooden hanger on the left. High, under-cut boots inlaid with jade-green leather in the tops stood tall behind her skirts and blouses. Fancy beaded gloves and gauntlets waited in the top drawer on the other side—handy at a moment's notice for a showy ride into the arena. Her spurs took a deep drawer where she also kept a hoof pick, brush, and curry comb for Harley. Her whole life for the last three years fit into the compartments of the trunk, other than Harley's tack and her rifle, which belonged to—

Unwilling to consciously recall his name, she closed and latched the trunk, then dragged it to the kitchen. Helen had returned to stir a kettle of beans.

"It's good to have you home. I was worried when you didn't come in last night. Now Kip says you're going back to town to take care of someone."

The woman spoke truth even if it pained her, and Grace wrapped her in a hug.

"We're going to miss you, Grace-darlin'. Seems like you just got here."

"I haven't been home long enough for you to miss me."

"You've been here all along, even while you were traveling." Helen stepped back and tapped her ample bosom. "Right here, wearing those pigtails of yours and out-shooting your brothers no matter how much they practiced."

"It's a good thing I didn't have a gun yesterday morning, or I might have taken an ear off a fella laying hands on the widow Berkshire."

Alarm filled Helen's eyes. "Oh, honey, is she all right?"

"Harley and I ran the guy off, and Doc Miller came and checked her over. He cleaned up a nasty scrape on her forehead and gave me a bottle of laudanum to administer three times a day." Grace chuckled and shook her head. "I doubt that's going to happen. But he commissioned me to stay with her a few days, and that's where I was last night."

Helen returned to her bean pot. "I appreciate you letting us know. Much longer, and I'd have sent your brothers to look for you." She swiped her forehead with a corner of her white apron. "You've got a good head on you. If the widow needs your care, I'm sure you'll do a fine job."

Mary came in the back door, her apron full of a garden harvest held bunched up in one hand. "Grace—where have you been? Surely you're not leaving again!"

The screen door slapped behind her and she dumped her apron-load on the table. Tomatoes, peppers, squash, and rhubarb splashed color across its smooth surface. "I thought you liked my rhubarb pie." She dusted her hands on the apron and pushed loose hair from her face.

"I do. I love it." Grace loved her oldest brother's wife even more than her cooking, and she gave her a heart-felt hug. "But I'm needed in town. Mrs. Berkshire fell and needs someone to help her for a few days. The doctor singled me out for the job."

"All that while Harley was being shod?" Mary dropped into a kitchen chair and began separating the vegetables.

Helen set two glasses of lemonade on the table, then took a seat herself.

Grace joined them, grateful for the cool glass and sweet drink. "From the livery to the widow's to the hatter across the street."

Both women stared blankly at her, inviting Grace to fill in those blanks.

By the time the tale was told, all three boys had returned, arguing over who would carry a large basket Helen filled with jam, towels, and medicinal supplies.

"Kip, take the basket and remember our deal with the harness," Grace said. "Jay and Ty, can you get my trunk to the buckboard?"

The two older brothers puffed out their chests and grappled with the steamer trunk. Surely, they couldn't damage it any more than a porter tossing it from a train.

"Perfect solution," Mary added as she filled another basket with a collection of the produce and pushed it across the table with a smile. "These might come in handy. Who knows how long it will be until you return."

The innocent send-off rang a sober note in Grace's heart. Yes, she'd only recently arrived and here she was leaving again. But not for places unknown. Cañon City and the widow's house were a mere ten miles from the ranch, but they offered the independence she'd grown accustomed to.

"Please tell Hugh what I've done and why. If it weren't such an urgent situation, I'd wait for him so he could go in with me and drive the buckboard home. But I need to relieve the hatter. I don't think he'll up and leave Mrs. Berkshire alone before I get there, but I don't know for certain."

"Hugh mentioned him a year or so back," Helen said. "Sounded like a decent fellow. He's caring for his sick father."

His father. Not an invalid wife. An odd mix of sorrow and relief shot through Grace, followed by a dash of shame.

After saying her goodbyes, it took only minutes in the tack room to find a short length of thick cotton cord. She tied a make-shift hondo in one end and called Kip to join her behind the barn while his brothers wrestled with the steamer trunk.

Kip watched wide-eyed as she built a loop and swirled it out in front of her, turning her wrist over and under, creating the wings of the "butterfly."

"Here," she urged the eager boy. "Hold the cord like this and turn your wrist." With her hand atop his, she took him through the steps a few times.

"You practice this until you get it—and I'm sure you will. You're a smart one."

Her praise lit his little face and he nearly grew an inch with pride.

"We'll work on some other tricks when I come back."

The butterfly went limp. "When will you be back?"

"I don't know exactly when, but I'll be back, I promise." She gave him a hug and pointed to a nail behind a small saddle on the wall. "Hang your rope back there, out of sight."

He nodded, catching the unspoken warning from one youngest child to another, then joined her at the harness.

They finished harnessing the mare the same time Jay and Ty got the trunk to the back of the buckboard.

"Good job, men." With her help, the trunk slid in and the boys fastened the tail gate.

"Let your dad know where I'll be. I'm sure he knows where the widow Berkshire lives, in the boarding house behind the feed store. Did you know your great-grandparents lived in the same house a long, long time ago?"

Three heads shook in unison.

"Well, you ask him to tell you. Maybe he'll bring you with him when he comes for the buckboard."

With Harley tied to the back, she climbed to the seat. Three stair-step boys watched her flick the reins and turn for the road. Two sad faces followed her movements, hands in pockets and shoulders slumped. But the shortest stood tall and nodded with a wink. Clearly the proud guardian of a very important secret.

CHAPTER SIX

Grace drove around back of the boarding house, where a light buggy waited—the same one that had been behind the hatter's shop that morning. Dan Waite had followed through on his word.

She unsaddled Harley, put his tack in the barn, and turned him and Barlowe out with the livery mare. Harley demonstrated his worth by rolling in the deep grass.

"A hundred-dollar bill for every complete roll," Cody had once told her. "Over and back."

She disagreed. Harley was worth more than money could buy.

Waite came out and dropped the tailgate.

Grace hurried over. "I can get this." It was bad enough that she'd begged him to sit with Dorrie all morning—after she'd accused him of not caring about anyone but himself.

Before she could apologize, he slid the trunk to the edge. "I'm sure you can."

The sting hit its mark, but she reached for one end of the trunk.

He grabbed both and marched toward the house as if he toted a hat box.

At the door, he stopped and looked over his shoulder, a clear signal for her to open it.

She snatched up Helen's basket, then complied, red-faced, judging by the heat dancing up her neck.

"Where do you want it?"

"Here in the kitchen." She indicated a space by the pantry door.

He cocked his head. "You're not staying upstairs?"

"Just leave it here." It really was none of his business. "Please."

"Suit yourself." He set it right end up as if he knew what it was.

From the parlor, a not-so-delicate voice called, "Who is it, Dan?"

Dan? Already they were on a first-name basis? She left the basket on the table and followed him down the hall to the parlor.

Dorrie sat comfortably, cup and saucer in hand. "Oh, Grace dear. I'm so glad you made it safely back, though you needn't have bothered. I'm fit as a fiddle." She pushed to her feet and the teacup slid from its saucer.

Dan reached for Dorrie's elbow.

Grace caught the cup. "The doctor said you weren't to be on your feet for a few days." She set the cup and saucer on an end table. "An order you have repeatedly ignored."

"Hmph." Dorrie swatted the air but sat down with Dan's gentle encouragement. "That old coot doesn't know what he's talking about."

Unable to hide a grin, Grace glanced up in time to see the shadow of a smile on his face.

"Well, the rest of us are fool enough to pay him for his opinions." Dan lifted her feet to the settee and covered them with a small quilt from the back.

His demeanor attested to what Helen had said at the ranch about him caring for his father. Shame burned through Grace, and she rubbed the palms of her hands on her skirt.

"Serving tea is not on your program either. You're not to be entertaining but recuperating."

"Ha! If this is entertaining, the two of you are harder up than I thought."

"I brought it for her." Waite grabbed his hat from the back of a chair, his voice smooth but unapologetic. "I'll be going now, Dorrie, unless you need something else."

"Thank you, Dan. And I'm sorry to hear about your father. If he's up to listening, tell him hello from one old soul to another."

His eyes warmed into a tease as he turned to Grace. "Let me know if you don't need my help with anything else."

Grace opened her mouth, but only the closing of the front door sounded. He had completely squelched her apology with mockery.

Her fingers clenched into fists.

"Don't let him get your dander up, dear. He can't help himself—he's a man."

Grace snorted and quickly covered her mouth. Dorrie's sassy humor drained the offense right out of her.

"It's dinner time." Dorrie drew aside the lace curtain behind the settee. "I imagine you're hungry, what with riding out to the ranch and driving back. That's two trips you've made in two days."

Grace lifted one shoulder and then the other, a relaxation habit from countless trick-riding expositions. "I'll fix something for us both. You shouldn't be taking that medicine on an empty stomach."

"Hmph." The widow adjusted the quilt on her feet. "I shouldn't be taking that snake oil at all."

She may have been hit in the head, but it apparently had not affected her wit.

Grace gathered the teacups and found it hard to believe Dan Waite hadn't used a mug rather than the delicate china. Definitely an uncommon man. But she'd known him a mere two days. He could be a ruffian.

Of course, she huffed on her way to the kitchen. Ruffians commonly had tea with frail widows, draping their feet with lap quilts.

She set the cups in the sink and filled the kettle, then squeezed around the trunk to check the pantry for biscuit makings. With a little grease from a small can on the stove, she'd have gravy and biscuits going in no time.

Returning to the stove, she pushed the trunk against the wall—another reminder of Dan Waite, who seemed to always be only one thought away. He'd known exactly how to set the trunk upright and would have put it in the outer room if she'd asked. But her whole life was in that trunk, neatly confined within its hard corners and, as meager as it was, she felt protective.

Soon the aroma of fresh biscuits drew Dorrie from the parlor before Grace called her. And she ate more than a bird this time, sopping up the gravy with the last of her biscuit.

"These taste just like your grandmother's biscuits, dear. Did she show you how to make them?"

Grace warmed with the compliment, pleased that a positive aspect from her past remained within her. "Yes, she did. But Mama helped reinforce her teaching. We didn't get into town that often."

"I pride myself in my bread-making, but Annie's biscuits were quite well known and favored when Cañon City was an upstart town. Potbellied biscuits, she called them."

Grace laughed as she pushed back from the table and cleared the dishes. "Yes, Mama called them that as well. Such a name."

"Your grandmother believed they led her beloved Caleb to her. In the early days, you know, when she and her father ran the mercantile and lived in the back room. They heated the place with a pot-belly stove, and she made fresh biscuits every morning on top of that stove. To hear her tell it, she kept freighters, miners, and other single fellas warm and fed that first winter."

Dorrie wrapped the remaining biscuits in a tea-towel and set them aside with an unopened jar of elderberry jam. "Speaking of single fellas, when you go thank Dan this evening, take this for his father. I suppose Dan could have some too since he'll be serving."

The presumptive comment left Grace trout-mouthed again. She clapped her jaw shut and cut soap curls into the sink.

"And that trunk is in the way. You could do worse than get him over here again to haul it upstairs for you."

~

After returning the buggy and horse to the livery, Dan eased the back door open and closed it as quietly as possible.

"That you, son?"

Blast. "Yes, it's me." Inside the cramped storeroom, he trimmed the lamp, then sat on the edge of the bed.

His father looked at him. "Is everything all right?"

No, it is not. "Yes."

"Tell me" —a sudden coughing fit wracked the frail body— "about it."

"One of my customers asked me to sit with the widow who runs the boarding house until she returned to take care of her."

His father peeked through heavy lids. "What's wrong with the widow?"

"She fell." Pop didn't need to know she'd been knocked down.

"Hit her head?"

"Yes. Doc insisted she rest, and Grace Hutton didn't want her left alone while she went to her family's ranch and back."

"Grace." A weak smile crossed his lips. "Good name."

Dan noted that half the crackers were gone, and most of the water. "You ate while I was away. Would you like something more?" Dorrie's bread came to mind, with fresh butter and hot coffee. Lord, bring the day that his father could enjoy such things again.

"No—" Another coughing fit.

At the dry sink in the back of the workshop, Dan emptied the canteen of mineral water into a glass and crushed a mint leaf in it. He'd used up their store of horehound, but the grocery would have some. Now might be the time to stock up on what they needed.

He helped his father sit up to drink. "Are you up to a little time in your chair?"

A nod. "Set me in front of the window."

Hope stirred.

It had been an early habit, his father sitting near the shop window, watching passersby. Over time it became difficult for him to hold his head up—until Dan got a high-backed wheelchair from the Hot Springs Hotel. It gave Pop's head a resting place when he dozed.

Dan helped him into the cane-backed chair, covered his legs with a lap-quilt, and rolled him to the front of the shop.

"What's her name?" Pop slipped his hands beneath the quilt.

"You warm enough?"

"That's an odd name."

Dan's chest cinched at his father's attempted humor. He didn't remember the last time the man had laughed.

"The widow. What's her name?"

"Dorrie Berkshire." Dan set him near the window and pointed toward the end of the block where the lane cut through. "The boarding house is back there behind the feed store."

His father hadn't been so conversational in months. Maybe he missed being around people. He no longer met the customers, and the last time they went to the café, a coughing fit forced them to leave before their meal came.

The only people he saw were others who took the waters or folks at the soda and mineral springs. They never visited.

"I'm going to the grocery. Wanna come?"

A slow head shake. "Not today. Maybe another time."

There was a fine line between coddling someone and caring for them with their dignity intact. "I'll be back soon."

He grabbed an empty flour sack off the sideboard, locked the back door behind him, and set off down the alley. Shaded already by the buildings along its south side, it'd soon funnel autumn leaves and a chill wind. He and his father had another winter ahead of them in the drafty storeroom.

~

Pop was asleep in his chair when Dan returned. It was too late to go to the baths, so he wheeled him back to his bed.

A can of peaches and another of beans made supper in the workshop. Leaning against the bench, he spooned out a bite of beans and considered his hat blanks. Grace Hutton had ordered a hat, and three times he'd missed a chance to find out her color choice. But it took little effort to visualize the shape of her face, her eyes, and that rope of honeyed hair. From coal black to bison brown and ecru, he had at least two dozen blanks of varying shades. What color would that spitfire of a gal want?

Several hours with Dorrie Berkshire, and there was no question about her color choice. Quite a woman, that one. Not near as fragile as one might think. No telling how many years she'd worn her widow's weeds. A warm brown or deep green might soften the lines around her eyes.

Soften. That was the word he was looking for. There was a softness about Grace—he'd bet his shop on it. A facet of her personality she kept hidden behind her bravado—until it came to helping someone who needed it. He reached for a fawn-colored beaver felt as a knock sounded on the door.

Irritated by interruption in the face of a clearly placed *Closed* sign, he found her there, hair plaited over one squared shoulder. Fortitude. No nonsense or flappery. Unafraid. But her eyes. Even through glass in fading daylight, they hinted of a mountain meadow in spring.

He unlocked the door. "Just the person I need to see."

Her shocked expression checked his wild-hare thoughts.

"My apologies. I was choosing a color for your hat since you didn't mention one yesterday." He stepped back, noting the bundle she held. "Please, come in. All my blanks are shelved behind the work bench there." He knew she knew that, but he had to say something that made sense.

"I'm the one who needs to apologize." A faint blush colored her cheeks as she set the bundle on the bench.

"I had no right to accuse you as I did this morning."

He'd witnessed both challenge and humility in this unusual woman, not a combination he'd likely find in many.

"Thank you."

She took to the chore without another word, touching a few blanks as if that helped her see their color better. Customers did that all the time. He even did it himself.

The fawn he'd set aside drew her first, and pride nipped at his good sense. She grazed a few others with a light hand, fingers gentle. After having his Wild West suspicions about her confirmed by Dorrie, he'd expected a firmer grip on the blanks.

The widow had filled him in on Grace's recent history, with a brief mention that she had out-shot, out-ridden, and out-roped both of her brothers since her pigtail days, as well as most of their rancher friends. Was that what had drawn her to the grit and glory of a Wild West show?

She returned each blank to its place before picking up a pale bone color blank. Much lighter than the fawn, but darker than the egg-shell hat she'd worn the day before.

Her choice, he predicted. But she set it aside and again lifted the fawn that complemented the shades of honey and sunlight in her hair.

"I like this one." She handed it to him.

"Well chosen." He set the blank at the end of the bench and with a pencil marked the inside of the crown with *GH*.

She moved to the other side. "I've come for two reasons. One, to thank you for sitting with Mrs. Berkshire while I rode to the ranch this morning."

He dipped his head in acknowledgment. "Not a problem" Though he'd thought it was at first. "I'm glad to see she's doing well. Has she said anything to you about her attacker?"

A disapproving frown drew Grace's brows together. "She did mention using a hammer on him if she'd had one in hand at the time. Frankly, I'm glad she didn't."

He chuckled. "I have to agree with you."

She picked up the towel-wrapped bundle and offered it to him. "Bread and elderberry jam. She said it was for your father, but you could have some too." A quick glance at the drawn curtain.

Was the bundle an answer to an earlier wish or a nosy intrusion? "So she told you I'm caring for my father."

Grace looked down and clasped her hands behind her back, then brought one around to her waist. "She mentioned him when you left, remember? But it was Helen, our cook at the ranch, who told me."

Odd that the ranch cook would know, but word got around in a small town.

"Thank you, and please tell Dorrie we appreciate it. He'll enjoy it, I'm sure." If Dan could get him to try it.

Grace folded her arms. "You can tell her."

"Excuse me?"

"You can mention it to her when you stop by. If you stop by. That was my second reason for coming." She turned her head toward the window. "Dorrie would like you to take my trunk upstairs."

If he didn't want to get to know this woman better, he wouldn't hold back a hearty laugh. "The trunk you didn't need help with?"

Like a whip's lash, her back stiffened and her jaw set.

"I'd be happy to stop by." Lord help him, he was going to choke on his own attempted humor. "An hour or so, will that work?"

"Yes."

At the door, she paused with her hand on the knob. "Dorrie also sends her regards, along with the biscuits and jam, and wishes your father a quick recovery."

If parting looks were grass-edged swimming holes, he'd be in up to his neck.

A brittle cough roused him from his stupor, and he went to the storeroom. Instead of sunken cheeks and lifeless eyes, pale blue greeted him from an upright position against the pillows. The first time without Dan's help in many months.

"What did she bring me?" Weak, but not as weak as before.

"You have the hearing of a barn owl." Dan laid the back of his hand against his father's forehead and found it cool and dry. "How do you feel otherwise?"

"Fine. And?"

"Bread. She brought you bread and jam from the widow."

"Well, let's have it."

Dan stared at the man who had refused real food for weeks, if not months. If he didn't know better, he'd swear his father was almost smiling.

CHAPTER SEVEN

Just exactly what Grace did not want—Dan Waite hefting her trunk upstairs with a smirk on his face. But lugging heavy loads was not in her repertoire.

"Is he coming over?"

Dorrie had met her at the front door with a broom in hand.

In need of something to do, Grace took it. "You're not to be doing chores, remember?" She started in the corner by the door. "He'll be here in an hour or two."

"You don't have to sweep the front porch."

"I need to, if you don't mind."

"That bad, is it?" Dorrie held her with a knowing look.

Grace walked to the farthest edge of the floorboards. "I don't know what you're talking about."

"You most certainly do. He's gotten under your skin as sure as a mountain tick in spring." The slap of the screen door punctuated her remark.

If you hadn't insisted I take him bread and ask for his help. The thought flew from Grace's mind like flecks of faded paint and dust at the end of the broom.

After finishing with the front steps, she set the broom inside the front door but went no farther. Instead, she walked around the outside of the house to the barn. Harley and Barlowe grazed in the pasture, and at her approach, Harley raised his head.

"Don't overdo it on that grass, ol' man. We're going to be here for a while." She combed her fingers through his mane and forelock, but he needed a good grooming. "I'll be right back."

On her way to the porch, she stopped at the wash room Dorrie had mentioned. Not comparable to the elegance of the Sheridan Inn and other grand hotels, but neither was it as dirty or cold as the wash basin in her tent between shows. A hardwood floor with a braided rug ensured that. But the pot-belly stove—that set her back. Had her grandmother cooked on something similar?

With Dan Waite coming to move the trunk, she hurried inside and went through its drawers and compartments, removing all of her tack, clothing, boots, and personal necessities. Harley's curry comb, brush, and hoof pick she set aside, and then took her Bible from a bottom drawer. Several notes and photographs fell out, and she pulled up a kitchen chair to go through them.

Nostalgia had a way of polishing the good times so they outshone the bad. As she fingered through the photographs, she traveled the miles in her memory and worked again with people she'd considered friends. Until she came to a postcard of the cast—principle riders, actors, and players—Cossacks, Vaccaros, tribal chiefs, warriors, and sharp shooters. Every costume was authentic, right down to the warrior's feathers and the chief's beaded headdresses.

Dottie "Deadeye" Dalton stood next to Lilly Mae Murphy with the opposite end of the line marked by White Feather and Captain J. Gayer, U.S. Cavalry.

Grace's eyes stung, pinned to the image of Captain Gayer—*Jackson*. His uniform was the only authentic thing about him, and it wasn't even his. He was as unoriginal as the scenes in which he played. And that's exactly what it was to him—play. He had lied to her from the beginning and she hadn't seen it. She didn't even notice what this photograph revealed until it was too late.

Tempted to toss the postcard in the stove's fire box, she slid it beneath the drawer and latched the trunk closed before taking Harley's halter and equipment to the barn.

The tiny tack room already held his bridle and saddle. An older saddle and harness hung on a side wall, gray and brittle with dust and disuse. Empty feed sacks slumped in a corner, eaten clean by mice and other critters. Too bad—she needed oats for Harley, but her remaining funds were limited.

If worse came to worse, she could take him home to the Rafter-H and let him live out his last days there with the ranch horses.

And that would crush her heart.

Halter and brush in hand, she stepped through the fence rails and into the pasture, pleased when Harley came of his own accord. Did he miss their traveling days, when miles clacked by on the railroads, crowds cheered and called their names as Harley bowed, his flaxen mane draping nearly to the arena floor.

He pressed his head against her shoulder, almost like a pet dog.

"I know, ol' man. But it was hard too."

She slipped the halter on him and ran the brush over his rich coat. Head low, he distributed his weight equally on all four feet, settling in for the grooming he always enjoyed.

The smell of horsehair and grass mesmerized her as she brushed. Was it merely the cleaning of his coat or was it the physical touch? The sense of belonging to someone who cared.

At least she'd come away with Harley intact, if not her heart.

"He's a beauty."

Startled by the deep voice, she spun around. Dan Waite leaned against the corral, one booted foot on the bottom rail, hat pulled low.

"Yes, he is." Harley hadn't alerted her, which was unusual. And she hadn't heard bootsteps. Was her horse that relaxed or did the hatter deliberately sneak up on them?

She returned to brushing Harley's shoulder, concerned that her horse would be so calm with a stranger. He'd always pinned his ears when Jackson came around.

"Where'd you find him?"

She knew what Mr. Waite meant but had to bite her tongue to keep from saying Harley wasn't lost. "We met in the show." She cut a look toward the hatter, ready for the next logical question.

"He appears to have a solid temperament. An admirable quality with all the noise and pageantry involved."

So much for logical questions. She stepped under Harley's neck and to his other side. "Have you seen a Wild West show?"

"In Denver, a few years ago. I considered joining up with Buffalo Bill himself."

She followed the brush stroke with her free hand. The country was peppered with people who dreamed of leaving the mundane behind and heading out for adventure and romance. But few followed through, and evidently the hatter was one of the many who did not.

"But I was younger then, before ..."

Glancing up, she saw his unfocused stare. Dan Waite's face was shadowed by his brim but still readable.

He blinked and looked at her. "Before responsibilities. Before we moved here."

Ah, yes. His father. "What brought you to Cañon City?"

A pinch of pain tightened his mouth. "When Ma died, my father took it hard, which meant the hat business also took it hard. Rather than leave him and the business to flounder, I stepped in. He grew weaker, and we relocated here so he'd be near the hot springs. I'd heard the waters were curative."

So had she, all her life. "I think they are to a certain extent. For some people, it's simply getting away from their lives for a while and resting. Relaxing in a dry climate. It seems to clear the lungs."

Sincerely interested, it was her turn to pose a logical question. "Is your father improving?"

Immediately she regretted it. Disappointment seeped into well-worn tracks at his eyes, and he looked away at nothing.

"No."

"I apologize." *Again.* "It's none of my business." She brushed along Harley's back, and with an arm over his rump, circled to his other side.

"Until today." Waite thumbed his hat up in the front. "When I got home—such as it is—he was sitting up in bed, awake and full of questions about where I'd been." A shallow chuckle.

"I'm guessing you live above your shop."

"Behind it, in a back room. Pop can't make the stairs."

Oddly, Grace thought of the screened-in porch. The invigorating fresh air. And how claustrophobic she'd felt at the ranch by comparison.

Rather than keep the hatter waiting and away from his father, she left the brush in the tack room where a shadow darted through a hole near a broken board.

"Thank you for taking the time away from your father, Mr. Waite. Please follow me and then you can be on your way."

He stood in her path, tall and solid but not intimidating. "It's Dan. Mr. Waite is my father."

"I see." Put off her center again, she hurried around him and toward the house, not quite ready to respond in kind.

Dorrie, on the other hand, had no such compunction.

"You've come, Dan. Thank you so much. I'm glad to see you found Grace. She will show you the way upstairs."

Turning to Grace, she added, "Your trunk can go in the room at the end of the hall, dear."

~

Dan gripped the handles on either end of the trunk and followed its owner up the stairs. It wasn't that heavy, just awkward, and Miss Hutton would have had to drag it up the risers.

At the top, she continued to a room at the south end of the building, kicking up dust and disuse as she opened the door. A pulled window shade muted the sunlight.

He set the trunk upright, turning the locked edge outward for easy access.

"Let me know when you need it brought down again, and I'll be happy to do it for you."

Her guarded expression didn't change. She nodded and led the way out.

Two more rooms were accessed from the hallway, their doors also closed.

Curious, he dared a question before returning downstairs. "Where does Dorrie sleep if she's not climbing the stairs?"

Miss Hutton took hold of the railing but faced him, speaking in a hushed tone. "She's using the study for now. It is a nearly hidden room, with access via a sliding panel door beneath the stairs."

"I see. She did mention that this was once a parsonage."

"Yes. My grandfather's, in fact."

Unexpected information. Was there more connection between the widow and Grace Hutton than he knew?

Dorrie waited in the parlor with her feet on a low stool, wrapping yarn into a ball.

"What did your father think of the bread and jam?"

The widow was a straight shooter, but he had work to do, so he welcomed it. "He sends his thanks."

"Why don't you bring him over for dinner tomorrow. It's a short jaunt across the road. Do you think he'd be up to it?"

No beating around the bush with her. He looked to Miss Hutton, who seemed as stunned as he was.

"You told me he takes the waters at the hotel two or three times a week." The yarn ball was growing. "This would be a much shorter trip, and the company might do him good."

Grace lowered her head and cleared her throat as if searching for words but finding none.

Dan palmed the side of his face, the stubble longer than usual. Why not come to dinner? His father had perked up at mention of the widow.

"I'll see how he's doing and let you know. Do you have a telephone?"

"Hmph!" Dorrie shook her head. "What do I need one of those contraptions for. Just clutter my house. I'll send Grace over before noon to see if you're coming. We'll be prepared either way."

He tipped his hat. "I'll see myself out. Dorrie. Miss Hutton."

She followed him to the door, facing him as an equal, neither flirtatious nor helpless. "You might as well call me Grace."

"No theatrical name?" Probably uncalled for, but hard to resist.

That eyebrow cocked again, as smooth and clean as a Colt .45. "Those days are over."

Well, there it was. A sore spot not to be poked.

He tucked a nod and took the three wide steps to what must have been a grassy yard at one time. It wouldn't take much to rake the fenced-in area, spread manure, and scatter seeds before snow flew. The old house could use a coat of paint as well, and a few loose boards nailed in place.

He and his father had lived in Cañon City for a year and he'd never met the widow Berkshire. Grace Hutton came to town, and he not only ended up helping keep an eye on the older woman, but now he and his father had an invitation to dinner.

On his way down the lane, he looked over his shoulder at the one-time parsonage.

A curtain dropped into place at the front window.

CHAPTER EIGHT

The next morning, Grace was up before dawn pinked the sky, stoking the bath-house wood stove and wondering if Dorrie Berkshire had lost her mind.

Dinner for Dan Waite and his father?

She turned the spigot for cold water and it pummeled the tub like a tinny waterfall. A large kettle of hot water warmed it considerably, and she added more of each until the water was half way up the sides of the tub. After letting her slip and wrapper drop to the braided rug, she stepped in.

Her hair hung loose down her back and she rubbed it with a cake of lavender soap, her favorite from Kansas City. Tucked into its small drawer in the trunk, it had perfumed her under garments and stockings as well. Just because she could ride and shoot like a man didn't mean she had to smell like one.

Ablutions completed, she toweled herself off, wrapped up her hair, and dressed in fresh clothes not as showy as before. Regular shoes, a plain brown skirt, and creamy blouse. Then she braided her hair and coiled it at her neck.

Inside, Dorrie was once more preparing breakfast.

"Good morning, dear. Are you ready for coffee?"

"What were you thinking?" Grace took a chair at the table, regretting her uncharitable attitude so early in the morning.

"Thinking?" Dorrie cast a smile over her shoulder. "I was thinking you should have a good breakfast before hunting down and plucking our dinner." A hot cake flipped into the air.

"I beg your pardon?"

"No need for that. Just scout around out by the chicken coup. It's attached to the barn, you know, and there's a hen that doesn't lay. She'll go nicely with green beans, mashed potatoes, and gravy."

A big chicken dinner on a weekday? "But it's not even Sunday."

"Tomorrow is and we can have leftovers then." Dorrie set a platter of hot cakes on the table with a small pitcher of syrup and gave Grace a compassionate look. "How long do you think it's been since those two men have had a home-cooked meal? There might not be any leftovers at all."

With a hand on Grace's shoulder, she added, "Better bring in two chickens."

What was it about this diminutive, black-clad woman who had Grace jumping to do her bidding? No one had ever had that effect on her except Mama. Not even Mr. Cody himself.

After coffee and hotcakes, Grace postponed her meal-gathering errand with a feather-duster from the pantry, an old tea towel, and a small bottle of linseed oil. She'd been wanting to clean the study since she found it dust-covered her first day here, and the parlor could use a good cleaning as well. Not to mention the kitchen chair legs, stair railing, and other visible items that collected dust.

But not the carpets. She didn't have time to dance with the Bissell carpet sweeper in the pantry corner, nor did she care to smell like a field worker when Dan and his father arrived. Enough was enough.

An hour later, she took a towel and the egg basket outside. She might as well pick eggs while she was out there, or Dorrie would when Grace wasn't watching her like a hawk.

She hated wringing chickens. She'd shot elk, deer, and marauding coyotes, but a bullet or even an arrow was not as personal as flinging a bird around until its neck snapped.

As she passed the open barn door, movement caught her eye. Another shadow darting deeper into the barn. Shadows did not move of their own accord, but she didn't want to chase down whatever it was right then. No telling what she'd find. A cat? Skunk? No, she would have smelled that critter. They always gave themselves away. And raccoons typically slinked around at night.

After filling the egg basket and ringing and plucking two hens, she was certain she'd never eat again. But Dorrie already had a big pot of potatoes boiling and two quart jars of green beans sitting on the counter with a slab of salt pork. They'd be eating chicken and green beans for days if those men didn't show up.

Grace dropped the birds into the sink. At least the house had running water, but only cold. This late in the year, it snapped like creek water on a winter morning.

"You'll find a sharp knife in the drawer there. You do know how to cut up and fry a chicken, don't you?" Dorrie studied Grace as if she'd recently fallen off a milk wagon.

"Yes, ma'am, I do. Why don't you go put your feet up and leave all this to me?"

Looking a bit forlorn, the widow rubbed her palms down the front of her apron and shuffled toward the hallway, pricking Grace's conscience.

"On second thought, I could use some help setting the table. I don't know where you keep your linens." She knew, but she also knew being needed was as important as being fed and cared for.

"And do you do anything special with your chicken?"

Again, the look of astonishment, but Dorrie went to the pantry and returned with a tablecloth, napkins, and a bread basket.

"Buttermilk's in the spring house. You know where the lard and flour are. Dredge it, dip it, and fry. And don't forget the salt and pepper."

Grace rolled her lips to keep from laughing and set to cutting up the chickens and changing the subject. "Do you have a black barn cat?"

"Not exactly. There's a skinny old thing that slinks around. It probably followed you with those dripping chickens and you didn't even know it."

The knife stopped halfway to a leg and thigh joint.

"Black as a moonless night, and if it is a moonless night, then you can't see it at all." Dorrie set four place settings as confidently as if she saw the men making their way across the street.

"Do you feed it?"

"If I have scraps, which never amount to much, so I count on it being a mouser."

Dorrie retrieved an extra knife, sliced bacon and an onion into a large skillet, and pushed it to the back of the stove for cooking closer to dinner time. "I imagine it scavenges along the few houses down the road, or behind the café."

"Have you named it?"

Dorrie shook her head. "No sense getting attached to something that won't get attached to me."

Grace winced. The widow's words cut with deadly precision, like the Bible passage that mentioned dividing bone and marrow. That was exactly what Grace had done—attached to something that never attached to her, though she'd been raised to know better.

"Don't forget the biscuits."

Grace looked up from her cutting board. "What biscuits?"

"Oh, didn't I mention it?" Dorrie rinsed her hands in the sink and dried them on her apron. "I'd like you to make your biscuits for dinner today. Maybe they'll have the same effect on Dan and his father as they did on your grandfather all those years ago."

~

After a two-hour nap, Daniel Waite, Sr. pushed up in his narrow bed, scooting back against the pillows.

"Dinner, you say?"

Dan marveled at his father's response. Were visits to the hot springs finally making a difference in his health, or was it hope for a home-cooked meal? Or visiting two neighbors he'd not met?

Whatever the reason, it didn't matter. Emotional causes often prompted physical responses and vice versa. Dan helped his father clean up and change his clothes, then padded the wheelchair for a trek across the street to the boarding house.

He changed his own shirt, polished his boots, and chose his best hat. Odd to go to such trouble for a mere meal. He didn't spruce up for his twice-weekly dinner at the café. Nor did his father ever eat the servings Dan brought home to him. Other than Dorrie's bread and jam.

Could it be that the mere suggestion of a woman's presence made a difference in a man's life?

His mother had—in both his and his father's lives—and it had been a slow decline since she passed. Even his own hopes for a wife had weakened.

The front door opened and closed, and he peeked around the curtain. Horatio Tucker had come for his hat—a smooth-top gray derby.

"Mr. Tucker." Dan met him in the shop and retrieved the derby from the shelf of finished hats. He gave it a final pass with a soft brush, an unneeded gesture, but the act demonstrated a personal touch for customers, adding a sense of worth to their choice.

Tucker tried the hat and nodded into the swivel mirror on the countertop. "Good."

A man of few words, he paid Dan and left, holding the door for the Hutton gal as she approached the store.

Grace.

Dan's pulse ticked up. He tried not to watch her openly, but he liked the way her name fit her movements. Smooth and easy. Nothing unnecessary.

She glanced at his polished boots and quickly looked away. "You and your father are coming to dinner?"

"Yes, ma'am. We'll be there in a few minutes."

"Very good." She hesitated at the door, considering the hats lined up like felt soldiers against the wall. "Please, it's Grace. No *ma'am*."

At the door's soft click, Dan marveled a second time. Not a predictable thing about her.

He returned to his father and found him trying to get into the wheelchair by himself.

"Hold on, Pop." Bracing the outside of the right wheel against the bed, he set his foot behind the left and reached over to lift his father as he always did.

"I can do this."

Unfamiliar determination scored the words.

Dan maintained his position at the chair, keeping it steady, but held the left armrest and back. He couldn't stand there and let his father fall without being near enough to catch him.

Frail and unbearably thin, Pop pushed on the mattress with his right hand and gripped the chair's right armrest with the other.

Everything in Dan wanted to pick him up and set him safely on the seat, but he reined in the urge. His father's arms shook with effort, and Dan remembered his own first attempts at pouncing a hat.

His small hands didn't have the finesse of his father's, and his muscles burned in the repetitious labor, rubbing rough sandpaper over a hat body, but with the nap of the felt—never against it. Over and over, he steadily sanded, trading paper to a finer and finer grit until the finished product was satin-smooth. It took hours, days at first, much longer than if Pop had done it himself, but his father let him do it. He wasn't in a hurry. He waited and watched and laid a hand on Dan's shoulder when the task was finally completed.

The next time, Dan pounced the hat more quickly. And quicker the time after that, until he did it almost as smoothly as his father.

With a grunt, Pop pushed himself off the bed and fell into the chair. Huffing with the exertion, he jerked his head in a nod, and set his feet on the footrests. "Get my hat."

Dan turned the chair toward the store front.

"Just get my hat. I can do this."

His father was going to wear himself out before they got to the door, but Dan pulled the curtain all the way back and grabbed the hat—a brown beaver with a Texas crown. A slight dip in the front brim.

He held the door as his father wheeled through, then locked it behind them. "I'll take it from here." His father didn't have to do everything on their first trip.

He checked the street for automobiles and buggies and set out for the lane to the widow's house.

First trip. Was that an unconscious hope that this wasn't the *only* trip?

~

From the hallway, Grace watched Dorrie watch the Waites as they came down the lane and turned in behind the feed store. The little woman pushed at the pins in her chignon and pulled a few wisps of hair over her ears. Then she pinched her cheeks and smoothed her faded black skirt.

Grace clapped both hands over her mouth and ran to the kitchen, nearly choking with surprise and laughter. She wouldn't offend Dorrie Berkshire for the world, but the woman was well into her, um—into her—oh, what did it matter? Men were coming for dinner, men she must consider exceptional. After all, she had spent an afternoon visiting with Dan. Grace hardly knew him, other than his kindness and air of strength under control. His deep voice, wide shoulders, and incredibly rugged features. All right, so she had noticed a few things. He would have done well dressed up in showy garb. Female spectators would have swooned.

As the front door opened, she checked that her braid was securely tied. But she drew the line at pinching her cheeks. What did she care how she looked to their guests?

She brushed the top of her skirt and joined Dorrie, whose eyes lit with ageless anticipation, astounding Grace at the transformation.

"Good afternoon, gentlemen. Welcome. I'm pleased you could make it. I hope you like fried chicken."

"Hello, Mr. Waite." Grace offered her hand to Dan's father, a frail image of his son.

"The pleasure is mine," he said, his voice thin but steady. "Please, call me Daniel."

Grace led the way to the kitchen, uncomfortable at the absence of a proper dining room. Even the ranch house had one, but here, the kitchen must do, and would accommodate six in a pinch. Had her grandparents never entertained guests?

Dorrie indicated the head and foot of the oblong table for the men, and she and Grace set out platters and bowls, then took chairs on either side. A pot of coffee warmed on the stove, and a pitcher of cool water perched between the green beans and the gravy.

Surely Cañon City had bottled sodas at the grocery, but Grace hadn't thought of it earlier. Dorrie needed an ice box. How good a Hire's root beer would taste chilled by a block from the Cañon Crystal Ice Company. Their delivery drivers came this far and farther to the outskirts of town.

Once seated, Dorrie held out her hands to the men, so Grace followed suit, the older Waite's cold fingers so unlike his son's warmth and strength. Lord, she felt clasped between the past and present.

"Dan, would you mind asking a blessing on the food?"

Barely noticeable, his hand tightened in Grace's. No doubt surprised by Dorrie's request, but gentleman enough to do her bidding.

The timber of his voice dropped and Grace closed her eyes, letting the warmth of his words envelope her. She'd grown up saying prayers, but there had been few in the last year.

At a collective "amen," she reached for the platter of chicken and passed it to the elder Waite on her right, but his hesitation warned her to set the platter between them. As she took a piece for herself, he did the same, and she handed the platter across the table to Dorrie.

Dan's jaw tightened at the near embarrassment for his father, but she read a *thank you* in his quick nod to her.

His father's hands shook as he attempted to cut into the drumstick he'd chosen. Dan picked up his chicken and began eating it picnic style with his fingers. Grace did the same, as did Dorrie, and Daniel eventually joined them.

All through the meal, in and around their pleasant conversation, she was keenly aware of Dan's concern for his father. Yet he never offered to help him, and she sensed it was the right approach. The hat business had been the elder Waite's, Dan had told her. He clearly respected his father enough to allow him his dignity.

A good lesson for Grace where Dorrie was concerned.

"I'll have another biscuit if there's one left." Mr. Waite directed his pale blue gaze at Dorrie, who not only heard his request, but seemed to read more into it as she blushed and passed the biscuit basket.

"I've not had biscuits like these in I don't remember how long."

"Nor have I," Dan offered. He passed the butter dish to Grace with a nod toward his father.

She waited for Daniel to scoop out a spoonful and then returned it to Dan.

Dorrie caught Grace's eye across the table and winked.

Dried apple pie finished off the meal, and Dorrie poured coffee.

"A short cup," Daniel said. "I think I've spent what I had enjoying the pleasure of your company and this wonderful meal."

The little lady's cheeks pinked, and Grace busied herself clearing dishes from the table. She couldn't believe her eyes.

When his father finished his coffee, Dan stood. "Thank you both very much. We appreciate your kindness but should be getting back."

His father didn't argue and seemed to sink a bit more into his cane-back wheel chair as if exhausted from the hour spent there.

"I'll help you at the door." Grace hurried ahead to open it and held the screen as Dan wheeled his father through. "How will you get down the steps?"

He turned the chair around and stepped back, watching over his shoulder, until he came to the edge of the porch where he tipped the chair up on its back wheels.

"Hang on, Pop. Three bumps going down."

The elder Waite gripped the armrests and looked up at Grace with a wink.

Laughter popped into her mouth unbidden, and she covered it with her fingers. Then she scurried down and out the front gate, holding it for the Waites as they passed through.

"Thank you again, Grace."

Dan's deep voice settled against her like a gentle heartbeat.

"You are most welcome. Please, come again."

His father raised a hand. "Oh, we will. We will."

Standing at the old gate, she watched father and son disappear down the lane next to the feed store.

Was it really the biscuits?

CHAPTER NINE

Dan started taking his father to the widow's on Wednesday and Saturday for dinner, and to the Hot Springs Hotel on Monday and Thursday. Each trip found Pop a bit stronger and brighter of eye. Thank the Lord, the move to Cañon City was helping after all. And it wasn't only the water.

If not for Grace Hutton's insistence that Dan help with the widow Berkshire, his life would be on the same depressing treadmill as before.

He drew the curtain while his father napped, and went to work on Grace's hat. Merely holding the unfinished form connected him to her as he imagined her wearing a hat that most women wouldn't consider. What was it about Grace Hutton that made her want a cowboy's hat rather than a feather-and-lace topper from a millinery? He'd seen women in Cody's show and others—dressed like men, riding like men, acting like men. But he doubted Grace had that air about her when performing. Her femininity could not be hidden by costume or disguise. A walking, breathing contradiction of fortitude and gentleness. Basically, the essence of her name—Grace.

The front door opened and a suited gentleman entered, trouser legs stuffed in his boot tops and a high-crowned hat cocked to one side. Robert Thorson, director for the Selig-Polyscope moving picture company that had been in town all summer.

Dan set Grace's hat on the shelf. "Morning, Thorson. How can I help you?"

The director stopped at the counter, flipped each side of his suit coat back, and stuck his thumbs in his belt. "I need some hats as fast as you can produce them. I'd rather not waste time going to Denver, and a couple of my actors are very particular about their styles. Most of the extras have their own hats."

"How many do you need and how soon?" Dan knew the answer would qualify as both blessing and curse—a lot of work in a short amount of time with a big payout at the end.

"Nine."

He found a notepad and pencil. "Do you know the sizes?"

Thorson took a folded paper from inside his suit coat and laid it open on the countertop. Nine names with sizes, colors, and styles for each one. "One of our wardrobe trunks was offloaded at the wrong stop, and we have no idea where." He spoke louder than necessary. "Next week we're going to start filming our final three-reel picture for the year. How soon can you have the hats finished?"

Frustration raised its ragged head. If Thorson wanted ready-made, let him go to Denver. Dan didn't mass produce. Some things couldn't be rushed. Each hat was a creation unto itself.

He turned the paper, laid the pencil on top and pushed it across the counter. "Number them according to priority and I'll start today. I can't promise when I'll have them all completed, but I'll aim for two weeks."

Thorson was not happy, but Dan held his ground. It was a take-it-or-leave-it proposition that did not include leaving his father in the lurch. "I'll need to personally measure and fit each actor if they want their hat to be *their* hat."

Thorson's sigh mimicked a steam engine, but he numbered the names, then pushed the paper back. "I have a flyer for your window."

Not a request.

Dan picked up the list of names. "Sure."

The director took another paper from inside his suitcoat, unfolded it, and strode to the window, where he taped the colorful notice in place. "Contact me if you know anyone who can fill this bill. You know where we are—corner of Fourth and Main Street."

After Thorson left, Dan easily read the notice from where he stood, sunlight pushing the bold letters through the placard in reverse: WANTED: FEMALE STUNT RIDER.

It might as well have had Grace's name printed on it. He crossed the room and slapped his hand on the back of the poster. Why couldn't they put a wig on a man? Why did they need a woman? And what exactly did they want her to do?

As his fingers pulled at the top of the flyer, unease shot through his chest. What right did he have to keep this news from Grace when she was looking for work? He wasn't her father or brother.

But he didn't want to see her hurt.

What he wanted to see was more of her, not less. And watching her endanger herself in a three-reel flicker was not what he had in mind.

Shocked by his reaction, he smoothed the flyer's edge and went back to his work bench. He hadn't owned up to his feelings for Grace until that very moment. Now that the truth was out in front of him, he also saw the futility of it. He didn't have time for courtship. He was barely keeping things together as it was, taking Pop to Dorrie's twice a week, to the baths twice a week, keeping up with hat orders, and trying to squeeze in enough shut-eye that he didn't fall on his face at the sewing machine.

He'd tried courting once before in Denver, and it didn't work then. Why would it work now at his age? And what would a ranch woman like Grace Hutton see in a twenty-eight-year-old hat maker?

The memory of Rosemary Patterson's sweet face materialized —a young woman he'd known since his school days. He'd thought they could make a life together. But his mother's death, his father's failing health, and the sinking hat business left Dan no time to give Rosemary what she wanted and deserved.

Watching her later walk by the shop on the arm of a city dandy hadn't done him any good. He couldn't go through that again with a woman like Grace.

He wouldn't. But he could finish her hat.

He picked up the fawn blank, turning it in his hands, seeing the finished product in his mind and the way it would shade Grace's green eyes, tilted slightly to her right—

The curtain sailed across its wire and his father sat facing him, hair plastered back and his shirt buttoned all the way to his thin neck.

"Roll me down to the grocery. I want to get something for Dorrie."

~

Wednesday afternoon, Grace squeezed the shell off a hard-boiled egg. Only four more to go. Chopped eggs, pickled cucumbers, and onions for Dorrie's potato salad. This was not how Grace had hoped to earn her way. She could do this at the ranch with Helen.

"Oh, Lord, help me. Ingratitude is an ugly bird."

The underlined passage in her grandfather's Bible ribboned through her mind. *I know the thoughts I have toward you.*

Did God really think about her? Did His thoughts include good and not evil for her specifically? If He did have a plan, she'd sure like to know what it was.

She untied her apron and laid it over the bowl. A few minutes would not ruin a potato salad. Dorrie napped in her room upstairs, where she'd insisted on returning Sunday night, so the study was open to Grace's visit.

Pausing at the foot of the stairs, she strained to hear movement overhead, any stirring on Dorrie's part. Silence filled the old house, so Grace continued as quietly as possible. Thankfully, the slider door had been left open and she entered the study without it scraping.

The Bible was still open atop the desk as she'd left it before. Settling into the old leather chair, she felt a sense of passage, as if entering a hall of wisdom visited by successive generations through the years. She smoothed the pages on either side, the same pages in Jeremiah that had greeted her before, but this time she saw the inked notation in the margin: Isaiah 55:8–9.

Her skin prickled at the handwritten reference, as if her grandfather was sending her a personal message. Quickly she flipped the pages back to the book of the prophet Isaiah and read the verses:

For my thoughts are not your thoughts, neither are your ways my ways, saith the Lord. For as the heavens are higher than the earth, so are my ways higher than your ways, and my thoughts than your thoughts.

Disappointment sank into her middle. That was no answer. What did these words even mean? What had her grandfather found in them that was so important he would connect them to Jeremiah's promise that God thought about them?

She flipped ahead to Jeremiah. "Thoughts of peace and not of evil, to give you an expected end."

As soft as a whisper the directive came, simple and clear. *Trust Me.*

The words dropped like tiny pebbles in the pool of her soul, spreading ever wider to secret wounds of inadequacy, hinting that she was noticed. Understood. Loved.

~

"Cinnamon?"

"That's right," Pop said. "Your hearing gone bad? Dorrie told me on Saturday that she was out of cinnamon and her watchdog wouldn't let her go to the store."

Watchdog? Not exactly how Dan would characterize Grace, though he could see Dorrie Berkshire squaring off with her and losing.

Pop gripped each wheel of his chair and headed for the front. "You comin' or not?"

Dan grabbed his hat, then held the door open for Pop, who sat straighter than usual. As if he had a purpose. For all his father's bluster about keeping the shop open during work hours, he didn't mind closing it for a jaunt to the general.

Cañon City had three stores that sold groceries—local fruits and vegetables, beef, and canned goods. About anything people needed to keep a household running. The general carried all that and a few other unexpected things like saddle soap, oil lamps, and ice boxes.

Inside, Pop rolled to a stop in front of the long counter. "Where's the spices?"

An aproned clerk pointed to a rack of tins and Pop made a bee-line. If he kept up this pace, he'd need a lengthy nap before they showed up at the widow's for dinner.

Dan had wanted to contribute to the hearty meals, but his dry sink and canteens didn't provide much of a cooking prospect. He looked around, thinking his father might be on to something. What else could they bring?

Pop studied the rack like a kid studied candy jars. It offered every imaginable spice available, and Pop plucked out two tins of McCormick cinnamon and one of allspice. Dan didn't remember his father ever taking much interest in the preparation of food. But if he was reading the signs right, it wasn't cooking that perked up Pop. It was the *cook*.

At eye-level to some items Dan didn't see right off, Pop rolled to a display of square, orange-labeled tins. "Oreo Biscuits." He set two boxes in his lap. "Does a body good to try something new now and again."

Dan bought a small sack of horehound at the candy counter, some local apples, and a tin of molasses. Hoping Dorrie and Grace could use the latter two. He got out of the store for barely less than three dollars. Much more of this, and he'd have to raise his prices.

On their return, Dan noticed flyers in every store front they passed, bold and colorful, as if promising the excitement of a lifetime. By the time they made it to the hat shop, his jaw ached from clenching it.

"Why do we need two tins of cookies?" he asked as he unlocked the front door.

"You want some, don't you?"

CHAPTER TEN

Grace sprinkled paprika on the potato salad, covered it with a tea towel, then peeked down the hallway. Dorrie watched through the beveled glass at the front door and gathered her long skirt with a gasp.

"They're coming, they're coming!"

How could a woman her age be as anxious as a sixteen-year-old awaiting her beau?

"Daniel has something on his lap. Oh, I wonder what it is."

Grace joined her at the door and lowered her voice to a stage whisper. "If you're not quiet, they'll hear you and know you've been watching for them."

The little lady covered her mouth and moved back a few steps. "Oh, we can't have that, can we." She brushed her faded skirt and tucked and pushed at her chignon.

"You look lovely. Stop fretting." Lovely in her eagerness and youthful anticipation, but also worn. Those old black dresses had to go. A little color around her face would knock at least a decade right off of her.

On her way back to the kitchen, a quick glance in the hall mirror was enough to elicit a frown on Grace's own behalf, and she flipped her braid behind her shoulder. Updos had never fit in with her lifestyle and she couldn't bear to bob her hair. But what did it matter? She wasn't primping for either of the Waite gentlemen, though one in particular did seem to take up residence in too many of her thoughts.

She shook him from her head and looked out at the pasture where Harley grazed, swishing his tail at flies. Oh, Harley, dear Harley. His dark coat shone beneath the midday sun like brown satin. He was the only male she should be thinking about or spending time with. Life had changed drastically in the last couple of weeks, and she'd not ridden at all.

She palmed back stray hairs and tucked them into her braid. Her beloved gelding didn't care how she wore her hair. He was faithful and ever true, and it had been her experience that two-legged males were often not.

The grossly generalized judgment nipped at her heels as happy conversation filled the hallway. Dorrie made over what Daniel had brought, but he wheeled into the kitchen under his own power and stopped in front of Grace. Quite lively compared to his first visit.

"This is for you," he said as he set a tin box of Oreo Biscuits on the table. "It does a body good to have something different now and then."

"Thank you, Daniel. How thoughtful." Maybe those Hot Springs baths were working miracles after all. "We shall have some with our dessert today."

Dorrie twittered about at the cupboard, making a fuss of adding three spice tins to her collection. "Just look at this, Grace. *Two* cans of cinnamon. Now I can make cinnamon rolls for Sunday breakfast."

She slipped her arms around Daniel's shoulders and hugged him. "And I'll be sure to have some for you this Saturday as well. Thank you ever so much."

Daniel flamed to such a bright red that Grace thought he might be feverish, but the strangled laughter fighting for life on his son's face suggested otherwise.

Dorrie and Daniel enjoyed one another's company. Exceedingly so.

Grace bunched her apron and with it took the stew pot from the oven.

Dorrie filled four glasses with lemonade and set a basket of biscuits on the table.

"I brought a can of molasses." Dan added a jar of Grandma's Molasses to the table. "Have you ever tried it on biscuits?"

Dorrie stopped in her tracks as if at a gun's retort. "Molasses?"

"Why, yes. It's not bad when you're short on jam or marmalade. I think you've given us all your jam."

Dorrie's countenance blanched as rapidly as Mr. Waite's had blushed, and it brought Grace to her side. "Are you all right?"

"It's happening, Grace." Dorrie tucked her chin and turned away from the men, dropping her voice to a whisper. "The biscuits, dear." She reached for Grace's arm and her hand trembled where it touched her. "Your great-grandfather spread your grandmother's biscuits with molasses when they were starting out here in Cañon City. She told me all about it."

A chill skittered up the back of Grace's neck, and she squeezed Dorrie's hand as she turned to Dan. "Thank you for your thoughtfulness. I look forward to making gingersnap cookies."

"Not to mention snow-candy this winter." Mischief glinted in Mr. Waite's blue eyes as he took his place at the table.

The family atmosphere in her grandparents' home had grown over the several days the four of them had shared a mid-day meal. Two generations were represented, nearly three with Dorrie's anecdotes of Annie Whitaker. Grace's thoughts wandered to "what if" more often than not. Unhappy memories wasted away in present company, and she dared not imagine what might happen if the Waites stopped coming for dinner on Saturday and Wednesday.

Dan cleared his throat and set his spoon aside. "We may not make it for dinner the next couple of weeks."

Grace's spoon slipped from her fingers with a clink on her bowl and she quickly retrieved it, blushing in her own right as if caught thinking aloud.

"Whatever for?" Dorrie's voice sounded entirely too high-pitched.

Dan glanced at his father, then at Dorrie and Grace, drawing each one into his explanation. "I've been commissioned by the Selig-Polyscope director to make nine hats in the next two weeks. It will take every minute of the work day and then some to keep up with my current customers and finish the company's order on time. I expect I'll be working evenings as well. We will certainly miss your fine cooking." He nodded at Dorrie and Grace. "And we appreciate you feeding us as you have."

Dorrie straightened as stiff as her chair back and pursed her lips. Grace tried to catch her eye, but the widow did not cooperate. Dare she warn the men to duck? An ultimatum was about to fly.

"Might I ask if it is merely the time spent here at our table that cannot be spared, or is it the travel to and from as well?"

An odd question in Grace's opinion.

Dan shot a guilty look at his father whose eyes held only Dorrie in their view. "As much as we enjoy coming over and visiting, it does take several hours out of the work day."

"Well then." Dorrie gentled her voice and spoke directly to Mr. Waite. "I don't see why Grace or I can't come calling at the shop two mornings a week and bring you home with us for the day. Then Dan can come as he has time, share lunch with us, and hurry back to work. We will see you home a little later."

Grace watched Daniel's face fill with warmth at Dorrie's words.

Dan's eyes darted from his father to Dorrie and back again. As he opened his mouth to comment, his father got there first.

"I think it is a splendid idea, Dorrie. Thank you for suggesting it. If you can put up with an old codger for that many hours in one day."

Dorrie blushed *again* and fussed with tucking her napkin beneath her plate's edge.

"But the steps." Grace could not imagine herself and Dorrie pulling Mr. Waite up the front porch steps.

"Yes, Pop." Dan rallied, as if encouraged by an ally. "How will you navigate the steps?"

The elder Waite regarded his son as a young boy, it seemed, rather than an able-bodied, adult care-giver. "I'm sure you remember enough carpentry to build a ramp from the ground to the porch itself, long enough that the slope is not more than these two fine women can handle. Who knows, I may be able to navigate it myself if given enough good food and gingersnap cookies."

He indicated the tin of Oreo Biscuits relocated to the counter. "Hand me a couple of those if you will. In fact, pass them around."

Before Grace could scoot her chair back, Dorrie was at the counter scooping small servings of egg custard.

And Dan had assumed Grace's trout-mouth reaction.

~

Dan clapped his mouth shut, caught off guard by his father's rallying remark. Facts became clearer. It was not so much the healing waters that were bringing his father around, but the diminutive Dorrie Berkshire.

Was the woman a miracle worker?

Grace added two Oreo Biscuits to each dish of pudding, and conversation soon quieted to remarks shared between Pop and Dorrie. Dan felt like a fifth wheel on a freight wagon.

Grace kept her head down, but a quiet smile turned the corners of her lips.

He shoved a whole Oreo in his mouth. He couldn't afford to think about Grace Hutton's lips, smiling or otherwise. How had everything gotten so out of hand all of a sudden?

"Leave the dishes to me, Dorrie." Grace rose and began clearing the table. "You and Mr. Waite can visit in the parlor for a while."

Dan finished his lemonade and took his glass to the sink. "Thank you for another fine meal."

Grace sent him a side glance as she shaved soap curls into the sink. "Could you please set that large kettle over the front burner and add a little wood to the fire box?"

Happy for a task that didn't involve shoving his hands in his pockets, Dan stoked the fire and moved the kettle. "Do you know if Dorrie has any lumber lying around, or something that could be dismantled and the boards used for a ramp?"

"So you're agreeable to the arrangement."

Not a question. Was she testing him or looking for an ally? "Are you?"

Her shoulders dropped with a sigh. "You see what's going on, don't you? At least I thought you did earlier."

She added hot water to the sink and sloshed it around with a rag.

He turned his back to the counter and leaned against it, watching her complete the mundane task of washing dishes, but more importantly, watching her reaction to the conversation. "What I see is what's happened to my father. Since we've been coming for dinner, he's returned to life. He's made a choice to participate again. Somehow, he's found hope."

Grace's brows flicked together then quickly relaxed.

"Does it bother you?" he asked.

She filled the stew pot with water and set it aside on the counter, then drained the sink and squeezed out the rag. Turning to him, she dried her hands on her apron, her green eyes full of tenderness.

"No, it doesn't bother me. I find it rather sweet."

The tightness in his chest eased, and muscles in his shoulders and neck relaxed.

"However—" Tenderness hardened to emerald glass. She crossed her arms. "I don't want to see her hurt."

He tensed, spread his stance, and held her cat-like challenge. "Nor do I want to see my father hurt."

For an airless moment, her soul stood up to him and his to her. Each was willing to fight for one they loved, determined to protect them, regardless of the cost.

Grace glanced away and back, worry displacing warning. "Do you expect that to happen?"

Her question brought breath to his lungs again, the softness he had suspected making an appearance.

"No." Risking a rebuff, he touched her arm. "I believe my father is quite smitten and revels in the company of another 'old soul,' as Dorrie put it."

Grace did not jerk away or scowl at his touch, though her eyes darkened and she looked aside. "They're lonely for companionship with someone their own age."

Was her remark a two-edged sword cutting toward herself as well?

He wanted to say more. Do more. Draw her into his arms and assure her that neither he nor his father would ever hurt her or Dorrie.

Good sense won over. He withdrew his hand and tipped his head toward the door. "Care to join me in hunting material for a ramp?"

As if relieved, she answered with a breathy laugh. "Yes, thank you. We may be surprised at what we find out there."

Dan held the back door open for her and followed her to the pasture. Her gelding had the place to itself, and the smell of warm grass and sunshine drew Dan to childhood summers long gone. Full-leafed cottonwoods stood sentry behind the barn, rustling with a breeze. A few more weeks, and they'd be as yellow as their aspen cousins in the mountains.

"Let's look around the barn," Grace said. "There might be something left over from the bath house."

The chicken coop opened off the east end of the barn, and a stack of weathered boards laid nearby.

Dan lifted one end of a long two-by-four and held it at eye level, peering down its length. "The front porch is higher than the back, three risers up from the yard. The back is only two. That would lower the angle and shorten the length needed for a manageable ramp."

Grace looked in that direction, as if she could visualize it through the barn that blocked their view. "That might be more feasible."

She reached for a similar board, turned it over, and jumped back with a scream.

Instinctively he stepped in front of her, forcing her back. "What is it—a snake?" He hadn't worn a sidearm since he'd moved to Main Street. Foolish, for the critters could be found almost everywhere outdoors.

"No—no, but—there." Hiking her skirt, she shuddered and pointed at a shiny black orb with eight spindly legs and a nearby egg sac.

A puff of air left his lungs, but laughter stuck in his throat at the look on her face. His mama didn't raise no fool.

One press of his boot heel dispatched the spider and any future generations related to it.

Pale and shaken, Grace snapped out her skirt, chin up and jaw tight.

He scraped off the spider's remains and laid the board with the one he'd set aside. "I would have bet my best hat that you aren't afraid of anything."

"And you would have won most bets." Light-heartedness had fled. "But if it has more than four legs, I'd rather not make its acquaintance. I met entirely too many such creatures in my travels with the Wild—"

She shot him a side glance and walked toward the barn. "Can you use shorter boards? I'll check in here."

"Your friends may be hiding in there too, you know." At least he didn't have to swallow his chuckle.

From inside the shadowy building came a dusty reply. "They are *not* my friends!"

A half hour of sorting and separating netted enough boards for a frame, several shorter pieces for braces and uprights, and three more black orbs bearing red hourglasses.

He didn't mind playing the hero's role at all, though Grace never voiced her opinion. She just looked at him with gratitude and made him realize he'd swim a raging current if it meant winning her smile.

He was in way over his head.

"I'll check at the lumber yard for panels. Maybe they have some of that three-ply veneer wood that was so popular at Portland's World Fair a few years ago."

Together they stacked the usable boards against the back porch.

"I thought we'd see the shadow this afternoon, but it may come around only in the mornings."

Dan sleeved his forehead. "Shadow?"

"A cat slinks around here sometimes. I've seen it twice, like a shadow with legs. Dorrie said she feeds it scraps but doesn't know where it belongs."

Grace went up the steps ahead of him and at the screen door mumbled something under her breath.

He could have sworn she said, "A lot like me."

CHAPTER ELEVEN

Grace sat at the kitchen table with pencil and paper. *Dress* joined her list at the very bottom.

Not on the list at all, yet by far the most important thing Grace needed was a job. A paying job. Not full-time, of course now that she was helping Dorrie. But she needed an income. The drawstring pouch in her nightstand drawer shrank each week.

"I see you're making a grocery list." Dorrie swept into the kitchen like a queen, noticeably lighter of heart and foot ever since Dan finished the ramp to the back porch. Saturdays and Wednesdays were the most cheerful days of the week, and the most labor intensive. But they were worth the extra effort.

Dorrie had a new lease on life.

"I'm leaving in a few minutes. Let me know if you need anything from the grocery or general."

Dorrie peered into the flour canister. "We need more flour."

"Already on the list."

"You're on top of things, aren't you, Grace dear." The old soda tin on the window sill gave up several coins to Dorrie's search. "Here. Use this. The grocer runs a sale on Friday, so be sure to check for other good buys we can make use of. And there's an extra nickel for the delivery boy."

Even twelve-year-olds had work. It wasn't fair.

Grace always dressed up when she went to town—a whole two blocks away. But it made her feel brighter. It didn't matter that most other women stared at her high-top boots and riding skirt. She'd not conform to the fashion dictates of city women. One more aspect of not blending in.

Her final remark last week about the cat had cut through her quite by surprise. Hopefully Dan hadn't heard it. She may not slink around looking for food like the shadowy feline, but did she belong here?

Sometimes she felt she did. Other times, she wasn't so sure.

Taking her purse and pride in hand, she set out for the dress shop first, where she was met with raised eyebrows and whispers aside. No sense seeking employment in such an establishment. However, she chose a deep green dress that would bring out the color in Dorrie's cheeks without her pinching them into bruises. And the collection of underskirts and corset covers was worth remembering.

Grace passed by the rouge and face powders. Dorrie would have the vapors.

The grocer was next, and he had no work for her. But she managed to snag a young boy to cart her purchases home. She stopped at the newspaper office and again found no work. That left one final stop—the hatter.

Not that she needed to see Dan. He would have let her know if her order was ready. But she *wanted* to see him, and that sensation quickened her breath. They had enjoyed many afternoons visiting, and he was proving to be a man of his word with no pretense. But more than that, his sense of duty and family were evident in his care for his father.

And when he had touched her arm that day in the kitchen, he'd been neither forward nor tentative. Controlled strength—a most compelling attraction. It stirred her.

A certain cavalryman's image faded into tatters.

Stopping short of the door, she focused beyond the glass to see him inside, working at his bench. He looked up, and a smile spread across his handsome face and right into her heart. Could he be as different from other men as she suspected?

Her own smile widened as she reached for the door and stopped short. There, in the corner of her eye on the glass to her left, a green and orange flyer with bold lettering called for a woman stunt-rider, sought by the Selig-Polyscope moving-picture company. Her smile froze as did her boots to the sidewalk.

How long had the flyer been in Dan's window? Were flyers also at the newspaper and grocery, and she'd missed them?

Dan hadn't mentioned anything about this in spite of knowing she was looking for work. Was he never going to tell her about a job tailor-made for her?

She blinked and refocused on the man inside whose face betrayed her revelation. He hurried toward the door.

She turned and fled, clutching the package for Dorrie.

"Grace—wait!"

A stitch pulled beneath her ribs at what he said, but she didn't stop.

Had he heard his words? Did he hear the irony?

She ran. From his words. From the possibility. From a name she was never intended to hear.

~

Dan watched until Grace ran out of view behind the feed store. In his mind's eye he saw her passing through the gate, up the front porch steps, and inside.

Hope slammed as solidly as the old beveled-glass door must have.

Why hadn't he told her?

Tomorrow's dinner would be more than awkward.

If he went.

His father rolled in from the back room and stopped at the sewing machine.

"You going to stand there all day or finish the sweatband in this hat?" He laid a thin leather strip inside a nearby hat, lined up the needle, and turned the wheel until the treadle went to work beneath his foot.

Dan returned to the work bench where six hats awaited shaping. He picked up a slate gray and began the hand-creasing process. "You up to taking the waters today?"

"Nope."

Smooth as silk, Pop stitched the band into the other hat, then trimmed the thread and set the form aside. "You didn't tell her, did you?"

His father's skill and dexterity amazed him—years of challenge and struggle honing his trade. But the way Pop read his mind and affairs was unnerving.

"You going to?"

Flat-out irritating.

He looked at the elder craftsman who held his head with determination.

"What's to tell? She read the flyer." When had his father read it?

Pop slipped on a pair of old spectacles and fiddled with the machine, changing out thread that didn't need changing, setting the stage for important conversation that always took place side by side, never eye to eye. Dan had always appreciated that trait in his father. As though they were equals just chewing over the meat the world threw at them rather than a father rebuking his son for biting off more than he could swallow.

"It might be a prickly trail getting there, but you don't want that woman gettin' away, son. You might try apologizing."

In four strides, Dan crossed to the opposite side of the narrow shop, both hands clawing through his hair, digging at images he tried to unsee.

"So I apologize for being concerned over her safety? For not wanting her to get hurt in some harebrained stunt the director might get her to try?"

He spun around to find his father still working with a thread spool, peering into the machine's moving parts through the round eye-glasses he wore for close-up work.

"She might surprise you."

"Yes, she might. Like slamming the door in my face."

Pop glanced up, nailing Dan over the top of his spectacles. "Like seeing that you care enough about her to be worried."

~

Grace shoved the package under the nightstand in the porch room and flopped across the bed. Angry tears raged to break free, but she refused to cry over another man. Again, she'd fallen for attention, kindness, and sense of belonging.

"Why didn't he tell me?" Recoiling from the pathetic tone of her words in the tiny space, she sat up. She was not helpless. She'd see this through. A clean face and freshly braided hair would do wonders for her appearance. And her hat. She'd look the part when she got there.

A knock at her door.

Grace jumped up and opened it to Dorrie, whose brows drew together in concern.

"Are you all right, dear? I heard you come in while I was upstairs."

"Yes, I'm fine." She closed her door behind her and led the way into the kitchen. "I see the delivery boy came. Did he bring everything inside for you?"

Dorrie chuckled and retied her apron strings. "Yes, well, in a way. It took both of us to get the flour inside. Those bags are so heavy, you know."

Guilt hammered a couple of nails into Grace's conscience. "I'm sorry I dallied. I should have been here to help." If she hadn't gone to the hatter's, she'd have been home sooner. If she hadn't gone to the hatter's, she wouldn't know about the flyer.

"Nonsense, child. We did just fine."

Grace splashed cold water on her face, dried her hands on a towel and finger-combed her hair for rebraiding. "I learned of a job and I'm going there now to apply for it. Will you be all right here by yourself?"

Dorrie hmphed and swatted the air. "I'm fine as bone china, dear. Tell me, what is the job?"

Grace didn't have the time or desire to go into details. "I need to be on my way, but I'll tell you all about it when I return." She planted a kiss on the dear woman's cheek. "No heavy lifting while I'm gone. Agreed?"

"Give me that hat. You've a spot that I can remove with a bit of cornstarch."

Appeasing the woman, Grace handed it over and went to the hall mirror to check her appearance from the waist up.

Dorrie was as good as her word and returned a cleaner hat.

"Thank you. I'll be back soon."

Stalling, she questioned whether she should take the time to groom and saddle Harley, or just go to the studio.

A knock on the front door interrupted her stewing, and she nearly choked at the outline of Dan Waite on the other side.

"Dorrie, if you don't mind answering the door, I'll be on my way."

Without waiting for Dorrie's answer, Grace hurried out the back and around the house, stopping out of sight until she heard the front door open and Dan enter. Then she headed for the studio at Fourth and Main.

CHAPTER TWELVE

Several people stood on the sidewalk and in the street, all dressed like participants in a Wild West show. But no Cossacks—the Georgian horsemen who could ride the ground right out from under anyone this side of the Atlantic Ocean. Most were cowboys in tall hats and oversized spurs, woolly chaps and batwings, all part of the moving picture company's production. Others were area ranchers Grace had known as a kid, earning money on the side. They didn't seem to recognize her.

One woman was mounted on a fine bay that reared at a passing automobile's rackety cough. The gal handled her horse well, and Grace's heart sank. She should have taken the time to saddle Harley. This woman was clearly there to apply for the female stunt-rider position, if she hadn't landed the job already.

"All right everyone, let me have your attention."

A suited man in a cowboy hat held a megaphone to his mouth. "If you are here to audition for the female stunt rider, move to the sidewalk in front of the studio. Everyone else, back up, either down the sidewalk or over here on Fourth Street."

Several women gathered in front of the studio door, including the woman on horseback who dismounted and ground-tied her horse at the curb. Frankly, Grace was surprised by the number of women there, who all apparently knew about the job before she did. Her fingers balled into fists at the thought of Dan not telling her.

But was it his job to keep her informed of what went on in town? She rolled her shoulders, stretched her neck from left to right, and flexed her hands. She didn't need to be tied up in knots.

And she didn't need a man to tell her which way the wind blew.

"You—what is your name and where do you live?"

A bobbed-hair gal at a folding table in front of the studio window waved Grace closer. "Well? You here to try out?"

"Yes—yes, I am. Grace Hutton. Currently I'm staying in town at the widow Berkshire's boarding house. Behind the feed store."

"Do you have an address?" The woman held her pen at the ready.

"I don't know it, but I can find out."

Deadpan.

"It's right across the street from the livery. My horse is pastured out back."

The gentleman with the megaphone approached and gave Grace a bold once-over from her under-cut boots to the brim of her hat. "Did you say your name was Hutton?"

She raised her chin. "Yes, sir. Grace Hutton. I've ridden with Bill Cody's Wild West and Congress for the last three years."

Conversations around her suddenly ceased, and the bobbed-hair woman and suited gentleman watched her with a mix of doubt and expectation.

"You don't say."

Addressing the man, Grace cocked her head slightly and planted both hands at her waist. "Oh, but I do."

A grin pulled one side of his mouth and he pushed up the front of his hat. "What can you do?"

Drags, lay-overs, running mounts, countless tricks, trips, and stunts dashed through her mind like so many scurrying mice. She chose a broader tact.

"What do you need?"

Her answer elicited a full-blown smile, and he offered his hand. "Robert Thorson, director. Did I hear you say your horse was nearby? Same horse you rode for Cody?"

"Yes, sir, on both counts. Would you like to see what we can do?"

"Indeed I would. Can you be back here with your horse in twenty minutes?"

That was cutting it close, but Grace took a chance. "Is there someone who can give me a lift in their automobile? I'm at the other end of town."

Thorson turned and waved an arm. "Freddie! Give the lady a ride to her horse."

A slender fella with a notebook and snap-brim hat directed her to a green touring car parked nearby. "This way, ma'am."

Grace hadn't been in an automobile in months. Not her favorite conveyance, but when speed and time were an issue, they fit the bill. "The livery is about six blocks down on the left. You can drop me off across the street."

The driver pulled away from the curb and took off down Main Street.

At his seeming disregard for others on the road, Grace prayed he wouldn't hit anyone.

He stuck his right hand out without looking at her. "Freddie Richmond, ma'am. Assistant director and Thorson's gopher."

She shook his hand. "Grace Hutton, trick-rider, roper, fancy shooter, at your service."

"Dang, if you're not exactly what we're looking for."

Hope spiked at his enthusiasm, but Grace was well aware that she was not one of a kind.

"Several women were trying out for the position. One even had her horse."

"Oh, her? She's a regular. Molly Myers, a bronc peeler, as she likes to be called. She'd like the job, but she can't do what Thorson wants."

The livery was coming into view, and Grace's opportunity for information was almost gone. "What does he want?"

Freddie turned in the lane and stopped next to the feed store but kept the engine running.

Grace stepped out and closed the door, leaning over it to hear his answer.

"Can you walk on water?"

Freddie laughed and backed up. "See you at the studio," he hollered before heading up Main Street.

Grace didn't have time to fume over the assistant director's idea of humor. Harley was about to have the fastest grooming he'd ever known and a nice little jog down Main Street. It'd be a good warm-up for him.

She glanced at the boarding house and dipped her head—as if Dorrie wouldn't recognize her, or Dan, if he was still there. But she didn't have time for explanations and arguments. She had to look her best. Do her best.

She ran around to the corral and slipped through the poles, whistling to Harley.

His ears came up and he ambled toward her.

"Good boy, old man." Leading him inside the barn, she could feel her excitement transfer through her touch as it always did. His head lifted and his eyes brightened.

"This could be our big chance, Harley. I need your best performance."

A quick once-over—a lick and a promise, her mother would have called it—was all she had time for. Satisfied he was as shiny as possible, she checked his hooves and the leather strap modification she'd made to her saddle, then stepped up, thrilled to be atop her old friend again. Leaning down, she stroked and patted his neck, then walked him out of the barn into the bold light of day.

"You're going, aren't you."

Surprised, she flinched, and Harley lunged forward, arching his neck and prancing.

She calmed him with a soothing word, then whirled toward Dan. "Sneaking up on a horse is not wise."

"I wasn't sneaking. You came out when I walked up."

"I don't have time to argue."

Dan opened his mouth to say more, but Grace clicked her tongue and Harley sprang forward into an easy lope.

~

Why, of the few women Dan had known, was Grace Hutton the one to capture his interest?

Headstrong, Dorrie had called her. Determined to do as she saw fit.

He jerked his hat off and slapped it against his pant leg. He didn't need the aggravation. He didn't need the distraction.

Slamming his hat back on, he struck out for Main Street and the Selig-Polyscope studio at the west end of town. He didn't need to be there to pick up the pieces, but he would be. He couldn't *not* be there. He couldn't live with himself if something went wrong. Again.

Which was exactly why he hadn't mentioned the flyer in the first place.

He'd known she'd see it eventually—it was all over town. But he didn't want her hurt, blasted woman.

From a block away, he saw a crowd of people take off down Fourth Street like a flock of ducks. Two men jumped in a coupe and drove around the corner, and a few cowboys rode horseback. Grace wasn't with them.

Something was going on, and he'd bet his last full-beaver felt that she was somehow involved.

He picked up his pace.

The crowd amassed at City Park, watching a single horseback rider lope toward a clearing near the river. The flashy horse gave her away. But even from this distance he recognized Grace's poise and confidence.

What was she going to do? Some outlandish riding trick like those he'd seen at a Wild West show years ago? Did they let women do that sort of thing?

He scoffed at his own question. *Let* was not a term one associated with Grace Hutton. No one *let* her do anything.

~

Grace reined in next to Thorson. "Do you have a handkerchief I could borrow?"

He pulled out a red bandana.

Perfect. She took it with a nod, loped across the park to an open, treeless area, and set Harley into an easy walk, outlining a long oval. Leaning over, she patted his neck. "You remember, boy. This is just like always, except with a little grass. But everything else is the same. You can do it."

His ears swiveled back and forth between her voice and the landscape as he took in the setting. After two trips around, she heeled him into a lope and circled again, then one more time to impress the pattern in his mind.

Pulling her feet up onto the seat, she stood erect, back arched slightly as she flagged the handkerchief in Thorson's direction.

No one cheered or waved. Even from a distance she saw doubt on their faces. Boredom.

Releasing the handkerchief to flutter down, she dropped into the seat and secured her right foot in the hidden loop. As Harley came around the far end of the oval, she signaled him into a free run, and with a flourish of helplessness, slipped from the saddle and hung by her foot.

Someone screamed.

Dangling with her other foot in the air, her heart pounded in time with Harley's hoofbeats. Adrenaline flooded her veins.

Her fingers dragged through the thin grass. The handkerchief was approaching in one … two …*snatch*!

She reached up and pulled herself into a sitting position, slowed Harley, and turned toward the crowd. On cue, Harley reared and pawed the air, and Grace twirled the bright red bandana.

People cheered, applauded. Some jumped up and down, and others stood gaping.

At a regal pace, Grace walked Harley toward Thorson, cueing the gelding into a bow as she extended the bandana.

Thorson stepped up and took it, then with a formal bow of his own, said, "You're hired."

CHAPTER THIRTEEN

Grace saw him at the edge of the crowd.

There was no missing that signature black hat screwed down so tight his face didn't show from a distance. But she didn't have to be standing next to him to detect the set of his shoulders. His wide stance and folded arms.

Everything about him said "mad."

"Miss Hutton."

She turned toward Thorson.

"We need to talk salary. Will you join me for dinner at the café?"

She stepped off Harley and gathered his reins. "After I tend to my horse."

"I'll have Freddie see to him for you." He looked around the crowd for his capped apprentice.

"No, thank you. I'll take—"

Someone's hand pressed gently against her lower back and the other reached around her for the reins. "I'll take him for you. I know where he lives."

Dan Waite's deep voice and deeper eyes promised delivery on his word and something else she couldn't make out.

She hesitated. Glanced at Thorson.

Dan never looked away or backed down.

"All right, um, Mr. Waite. Thank you." She relinquished the reins.

"Ah, yes, the hatter. Of course you would know each other. Thank you, Waite."

Dan touched the edge of his hat brim and led Harley away from the crowd.

She watched them walk down Fourth Street to the corner of Main, where they turned right and disappeared from her view.

Dan could have ridden him. He didn't have to walk him home. Maybe—

"Miss Hutton?"

"Wha—yes?"

"Let's take my car, then I can drive you home later."

"I'll join you." Dark-haired Molly Myers flashed a glorious smile and maneuvered between Grace and Thorson.

"Molly, I'd like you to meet Grace Hutton." Addressing Grace, he added, "Miss Hutton, Molly Myers, a fine actress and horsewoman in her own right."

"Though I prefer to keep both my feet in the stirrups when I ride."

She hooked her right arm into Grace's. "Tell me, where did you ever learn such a stunt? It reminded me of the Cossack death drag I saw once in a Wild West show."

~

Dan's hands shook as he unsaddled Grace's gelding and rubbed him down. He couldn't stop the shaking, repulsed by the gut kick he'd felt when she "fell" off the horse. Even though he knew it was planned and backed up with the proper equipment, it had made him sick.

Oats were needed after a performance like that, but he found none and turned the horse out in the pasture before taking the tack inside the barn.

The underside of Grace's saddle was still warm from Harley's sweat and exertion, and Dan found the leather loop attached securely to her saddle that allowed her to pull off such a harebrained stunt.

He tried to shake off the clinging dread, the fear. He was no greenhorn. He'd seen performance drags before. Several times, in fact. But it hadn't been someone close to him. Someone he felt responsible for, like—

"Dan, are you in here?"

Dorrie stood at the barn door, frowning into the shadows.

"Just putting things away for Grace." He sucked in a deep breath and blew it out hard, clearing his head.

"I saw you walk by with her horse. Is everything all right? Is she hurt?"

Joining Dorrie in the bright sunshine, he patted her shoulder, gently indicating they go to the house. "She's fine. Did she tell you where she was going?"

Dorrie lifted her skirt and used the ramp rather than the stairs. "No, she didn't. She merely flew out the back door when you knocked at the front. What is going on?"

Wincing from the not-so-subtle avoidance, he opened the screen door and followed her inside.

While Dorrie set a kettle of water on to boil, he pulled out a chair and took his hat off. "She tried out as a stunt rider for the moving picture folks."

Dorrie tsked and shook her head. "I know she's completely capable, but dear me, what a thing to do." She took two cups from the cupboard. "Do you know if she got the job—if you can call it that? She doesn't need a job, if you ask me. She needs a good man."

A low-brow side glance sliced across his shirt pockets.

"I'm afraid she did." He rubbed the back of his head. "The director took her to the café to talk about salary."

"Oh dear."

A noise outside drew their attention to the window, and before Dan could get to the porch, his father wheeled up the ramp.

"Is this a private meeting?"

Dan opened the screen and stepped aside. "What are you doing here? We don't come for dinner until tomorrow."

"Says who?" His father rolled inside and around the kitchen table to the end nearest the stove.

Dorrie already had a cup and saucer for him and dropped in a tea strainer.

"Thank you, ma'am."

She cuffed his shoulder. "I told you, don't call me *ma'am*. It's Dorrie."

His father winked at him, then added sugar to his tea.

Dan's world was turning upside down faster than Grace had.

"Are you sure you feel all right?" He scrutinized his father's face. No red blotches. No sunken cheeks, though he could use a little sun.

"The only thing I need is conversation and a piece of pie." Another wink.

Dorrie opened the pie safe. "Who told you I had pie over here?"

"You did. On Wednesday. Said you were making a pie on Friday and too bad I wouldn't be here. Ha!"

Dorrie's face lit with a smile to shame an electric light bulb. Three small plates and forks later, each of them had a slice of canned-peach pie. "You're going to eat me out of house and home. I swear."

Pop jutted his chin toward the empty chair and raised his eyebrows at Dan.

Dan ignored the question and forked off a bite of peaches.

"Where's Grace?" his father said. "She's missing out."

Pop was resurrecting his old ornery self. The self that Dan had nearly forgotten, though he was grateful the man felt as well as he did.

"Your son said she was at the café having dinner with the moving picture director."

"Hmm." Pop swallowed. "How do you know that?"

Dan hadn't had so little privacy since he was a youngster living at home.

"I got over here as she was leaving for the studio with Harley, and I made it down there in time to see her ride across the park at the end of Fourth Street." No sense getting Dorrie worked up over *how* Grace rode.

Dorrie gasped and held a napkin against her mouth.

He gentled his voice, thankful he'd left out the *drag* part. "Don't worry, Dorrie. She's good at what she does."

"Oh, I know that, dear. I just hope she didn't ruin her hat. I cleaned it for her before she left. Had a smudge that came right off with a little corn starch."

Dorrie served tomato sandwiches and more pie, and a couple of hours of conversation waned into late afternoon. She and Pop sat outside on the front porch, and Dan wrestled with his own good sense, cleaning stalls in the barn that didn't need cleaning. So much for a day's work on his hat orders, but he'd be useless at the shop. Better to do whatever needed doing around the widow's.

He split firewood for the bath-house, cut kindling for the kitchen stove, and drank an entire pot of coffee waiting for Grace to show up.

What was taking so all-fired long?

He started a fresh pot and was rinsing out his cup when boots sounded on the back porch.

Through the screen door, Grace looked worn and tired, but when she stepped inside and saw him, distrust colored her face as well as her words. "What are you doing here?"

Catching herself, she hung her hat on a hook by the door and palmed loose hair from her face. "I mean—thank you for bringing Harley home. Did he give you any trouble?"

"None. He could use a can of oats, but I didn't see any around."

Grace dropped into a kitchen chair and rubbed her arms. "I can afford to get it for him now."

Dan pulled out a chair and straddled it. "Coffee'll be ready soon. Dorrie's on the front porch with Pop."

"I saw them." She crossed one arm over and rubbed her shoulder, then did the same for the other side. "When I walked past, they were engrossed in each other and didn't notice me. But Harley was happy to see me." She glanced at Dan. "Thank you for rubbing him down and putting away his tack."

"I know my way around horses. Never hung upside-down on one, but I've owned a few."

Weariness rimmed her eyes, and she blinked slowly. "Why did you take him? You weren't exactly cheering."

"He needed to be cared for." Like her, but he figured she'd put up a squall if he mentioned it. He'd suggest she soak in a hot tub if it weren't such a boldly improper thing to bring up.

Instead, he gave her the last piece of peach pie and offered a hint. "I filled the kindling box here and the one outside as well."

She looked at him, puzzlement drawing her brows together.

"In the bath house."

"Oh. Yes, that." Too weary to blush, she punched holes in the piecrust with her fork.

He feared she might fall right out of her chair. To blazes and back with improper.

"I'll start a fire out there for you, heat some water, and get it ready. I've had a little practice at that."

Her pride reared and she stiffened. "Thank you, but I can take—"

"—care of yourself. I know."

He left her with her mouth open, but she settled enough to finish the pie before he returned.

"Didn't you eat at the café with Thorson?"

"Not much. I didn't want to be beholdin' to him."

Dan nearly snorted, but wisdom won out. "He hired you, didn't he?"

Her face brightened beneath the layer of dust that covered her clothing as well. "Twenty-five dollars a day."

The amount shocked him. He was in the wrong enterprise. "Is the risk worth it to you?" None of his business, but hang it all, he cared whether Grace Hutton broke her pretty neck.

Her shoulders loosened beneath a weary sigh. "It's what I do, Dan."

Dan. Not Mr. Waite.

"And it's short-term. This is their last flicker of the season, but it will keep me until I find something more permanent."

She stood and pushed in her chair, hanging onto the back as she gathered her thoughts, then looked him in the eye. "Why didn't you tell me about the flyer?"

No anger edged her words or eyes, but vindication lay just beneath the surface. A gentlewoman's way of saying "I told you so."

He stood but held his place. "Because stunt riding is a risky thing to do."

A weary smile. "What isn't?"

"I didn't want to see you hurt." *Spit it out, Dan. Take the risk.*

He walked around the table and stopped close enough to smell horse sweat and fatigue. Close enough to smell his own fear and fall head-first into her green gaze.

"I didn't tell you because I didn't want to lose you like I lost someone else I cared about."

CHAPTER FOURTEEN

Dan Waite was right. A hot bath was exactly what Grace needed, and he wasn't afraid to suggest it. In a manner of speaking.

She set her boots against the door and let her clothing slip to the braided rug beneath her feet. The stove put out a surprising amount of heat, and the sweet smell of cedar wood filled the small room. A towel and soap cake sat on a chair next to the tub. She loosed her braid and stepped into the water, sliding down until it covered her shoulders.

Heaven on earth.

Of the baths she'd enjoyed in a few fine hotels across the country, none compared to this rough-board shack, tin tub, and pot-bellied stove.

Like someone else I cared about.

As gently as the warmth seeping into her limbs, Dan's words seeped into her heart. Had he withheld information about the flyer because he cared about her safety?

Or did she merely remind him of someone else he had truly cared for?

A tiny sting to her pride, like water not cooled enough.

Two small windows high in the wall let the afternoon sun slant inside. Contentment had never felt so near. Harley was safe. Grace had a roof over her head, food on the table, and a friend who needed her.

And Dan?

It was too soon to tell. Their disagreement over her work too raw. Another man's betrayal too recent. And this man's words too vague.

She tipped her head back against the tub and closed her eyes.

~

"Grace!"

Startled by the shrill voice and rattling of the fragile door, Grace shot up, chilled by tepid water. She reached for the towel.

"Is that you, Dorrie?"

"Well, it's certainly not Baby Doe Tabor. You had me as worried as a toad under a harrow."

Dripping and drying off in the dark, Grace realized she'd not brought clean clothes with her.

"Dorrie, would you please do me a favor?"

"I've already done it. Got your clothes right here if you'll unlock the door."

How could Grace have been so scatterbrained as to forget a change of clothes? She wrapped the towel around her and opened the ailing door.

"I suppose I could have kicked it in, but I didn't want to have to replace it. Though I'm sure Dan could have handled it nicely. Here you are."

"He's not out there, is he?" Grace snatched the clothing and pressed it close against her.

"No, child. He's gone home with his father. But he's the one who told me you were in the bath house."

Heat flashed through Grace's body at the thought, but there was nothing to do about it. "Give me a few minutes and I'll be out."

"I'll put on a fresh pot and butter up some toast."

Peeking through the cracked door, Grace watched Dorrie go up the ramp rather than the steps and into the kitchen, enticing with its welcoming light.

Home. Not much in Grace's life had felt more like home since she was a girl on the ranch with her mother.

After coffee, toast and jam, and a general retelling of what she and Harley had accomplished, sleep pursued Grace upstairs in Dorrie's wake. The little lady perched herself on a padded bench in front of an old dressing table and started unwinding her topknot.

"Let me do that for you." Grace gently removed the combs and hairpins, amazed at the length of Dorrie's hair—brown at the very tips, but streaked with white around her face. "May I brush it for you?"

Dorrie swatted the air. "Oh, you don't have to do that. I simply put it in a loose braid. I don't think that one-hundred-strokes business does anything other than sell more hair brushes."

Grace chuckled at another of Dorrie's unmasked opinions. Beginning at the bottom of the long strands, she worked her way up, loosening knots as she went. "The last time someone brushed my hair, I was getting ready for graduation. Mama insisted she work out every snag before I put on my special dress."

The memory tugged as surely as the tangles had in Grace's mane of hair.

"You know, your Grandmother Annie's hair had a mind of its own. It wasn't as long as yours or mine, but oh, how it flashed in the sunlight, even in her widowhood. Streaked with gray, of course. That is hard to avoid when one reaches this side of life. How it shone, even then, when struck through with sunlight. Just like her spirit."

A drop of sorrow splashed into Grace's heart. "I wish I had known her better."

"She was a bold young woman for the time. And she never forgot her days of living in the livery stall or the back of the mercantile when they first came to Cañon City. Your grandpa Caleb did the same, you know—moved into the livery."

Grace pulled the brush through the full length of hair that reached to the padded bench. "Somewhat like Dan and Daniel today."

"Oh, yes. I dare say, she'd be pleased to know we are helping those fine men with a few comforts of home."

Grace believed the little lady was in love with the elder Waite, but it wasn't any of her business, in spite of how close she and Dorrie had grown.

"Tell me, dear, what do you think of Dan?"

Grace laid the brush on the dressing table and divided the hair into three sections, none too surprised that Dorrie had turned the tables on her again, as if she knew the inner workings of Grace's mind.

"That's hard to answer."

Dorrie watched her in the mirror, seeing more than most, but wisely waiting, listening.

"I fear I've ridden a teeter-totter in that man's presence. One minute I don't trust him, the next I want to know what he thinks and feels. He infuriates me too. Did you know he refused to tell me about the moving picture company looking for a woman stunt rider?"

Unsure how Dorrie would respond, Grace gave her a moment to comment while loosely braiding her hair.

She merely seamed her lips.

"How dare he not tell me, as if he was in charge of my life!"

Dorrie pulled the finished braid over her shoulder. "How dare he care."

Heat rushed up Grace's neck, flushing into her face. She dropped onto the end of Dorrie's bed. "That's what *he* said, in a round-about sort of way."

Dorrie slowly turned to face her. "He told you he cared for you?"

Grace picked at the quilt top. "Maybe. He said he didn't want to lose me like he had someone else he'd cared about." Unable to form words that adequately described her warring emotions, she felt as conflicted as a staged battle with attackers running rough-shod and rescuers close behind.

"Sometimes I think I wouldn't mind caring for him."

Dorrie's head tipped to the side. "Wouldn't mind?"

"All right." Grace's breath escaped like air from a popped balloon. "I could—no, I *do* care for him. I think."

Dorrie went to the other side of the room behind a screen and changed from her dress into a nightgown. Then she fluffed her pillows and crawled beneath the blankets.

Folding her hands atop her quilt as if preparing for bedtime prayers, she asked, "May I tell you a secret?"

Puzzled, Grace wasn't so sure she wanted to know the secrets of an elderly woman whom she believed was falling in love with a certain elderly man. "I suppose."

"It has been my experience that a tender-hearted man is a rare gift, Grace. Most men don't have the courage for it. They're afraid." She pressed back into her pillows, closed her eyes, and tugged the quilt a little higher.

"Dan Waite is not most men."

~

Dan wrapped a towel around the loaf of bread Dorrie had sent with him and set it next to a jar of elderberry jam on the counter. The palms of his hands tingled, and he rubbed them on his denims. A far cry from what he wanted to do with them.

He checked again on his father who was sleeping soundly—worn out, he guessed, from a day of conversation and wheeling himself across the road and into the house. That was as surprising a stunt as Grace dragging across City Park. But there had been no wheezing and no coughing.

Dan's conviction grew stronger that there was more of a miracle at work here than healing waters.

God, I need wisdom.

He checked the door locks and lit an oil lamp on the work bench rather than turn on the electric light. From beneath the counter, he withdrew his Bible and sat down near the lamp.

Opening to the first chapter of James, he read a verse he'd often turned to in the days following his mother's passing.

If any of you lack wisdom, let him ask of God, that giveth to all men liberally, and upbraideth not; and it shall be given him.

"Lord, help me not mess things up." The whispered prayer had accompanied many a hat when he was starting out. But this time it went deeper than a shapeless form. He could clearly see what was going on between Pop and Dorrie, but all he knew where Grace was concerned was what he wanted.

He wanted *her*.

And he wanted her to be safe.

His father had been right about telling her how he felt. The same way he'd been right over the years about creating the perfect hat for every customer.

Shaping a hat was a lot like shaping a relationship—knowing when to apply pressure and when to use a gentle touch. When to use heat, and when to smooth things over.

With that in mind, he'd promised Grace a hat before he contracted with Thorson, and he took the fawn-colored blank from the shelf.

His hands moved of their own accord, trained in the craft and confident in their skill. But his mind wandered to the amazing woman who had captured him so completely. It wandered further to how she'd survive winter nights on that screened-in porch. Temperatures would drop to freezing in a few short weeks. Would she move upstairs, where she belonged? Or could he board up the porch and keep it warm enough for winter?

He scoffed. Highly unlikely, with no door connecting it to the main house. It shared a wall with the kitchen, but that wasn't enough to transfer heat.

Grace had to move inside. And if he told her that, she'd sull up like a soured colt.

Twice he trimmed the lamp as he worked into the night, not watching the time, but lost in the creation of what he believed to be the perfect cover. It mirrored the slender curves of her body, with a gently sloping brim. Stiff enough to hold its shape in a hard wind, yet gentle in appearance, making him want to be the first drop of water that pooled in a storm and fell from its brim to the hand holding her reins.

If he kept this up—these dreams and visions of what could be—it wouldn't take much more for him to lose his mind.

His heart was already a goner.

CHAPTER FIFTEEN

"We've got a runaway stagecoach and we need you to chase it down, jump from your horse, and take control of the team." Thorson looked at Grace. "Dressed like Molly."

Grace stood in her stirrups for a better view of the incline ahead that narrowed into a razor's edge, dropping off on both sides about a hundred feet.

Was Thorson out of his mind?

No wonder Molly wanted to keep both feet in the stirrups.

"I can do it, but not here."

The director stammered into an irritated holler. "Why not?"

Grace swept her arm out over the scenic drop below them. "You are severely short on land."

He swore under his breath.

A couple of cowboys grinned, but silently.

"I'll chase the stagecoach to the top, then chase it down the other side, but I won't risk the life of my horse on this narrow sky-track. I'll do the stunt on flat ground and you can splice it in."

Since Cody had taken an interest in filming his Wild West Show the previous year, she'd learned about such scenes. It was entirely possible.

She also knew that no one else would do the stunt, so she wasn't surprised when Thorson swept his hat off and mopped his forehead with his sleeve. "All right. We'll shoot the chase now and tomorrow film the transfer up on the road to the Hutton ranch."

The cameraman jumped in the back of a roadster where his camera and tripod were set up, and outriders started up the incline.

"Regi!" Thorson hollered at the stage driver. "After this scene, rest the horses, then head for the Huttons'. I'll send someone ahead to ask if we can board our stock there tonight."

Grace heeled Harley closer to the conversation. "I'll go."

The director looked up at her, squinting into the sun. "All right. That might be best. They won't run *you* off."

Laughing at his own joke, he headed for the incline. "Places. Everyone—places!"

"Miss Hutton, come with us, please." The woman in charge of makeup led Grace to a car, where she and the costumer pinned up her braid, then decked her out in a black wig, chaps, and a different shirt.

Harley was good to go.

An hour later, Grace rode a lathered Harley down the backside of the hogbacks. "Good job, ol' man." She patted his neck, wet with sweat beneath his mane. "Harder than our runs with the show, but you're holding up well. An easy walk to the ranch will be good for your old bones. Keep you from stocking up."

It would be good for her too. Quiet time to think about all that had happened in the last few weeks. All the feelings that were coming to life inside her, emotions she'd sworn off and promised never to entertain again. All the things that she and Dorrie had talked about.

Dan Waite is not most men.

Dorrie's comment had pushed its way into a back corner of Grace's heart and taken a seat right next to Dan's remark about caring for her. Neither were as flamboyant and rosy as things Jackson had said to her. She snorted.

That should have been her first hint. Captain Jackson Gayer was all bluster. An empty cream puff—appealing on the outside, hollow on the inside.

The image was enough to set her stomach growling. She'd stop at Reide's Bakery on her way out of town and pick up some pastries for Helen and the boys. But first she needed to water Harley, brush him down, and let him rest a bit.

As she neared the boarding house, her attention focused on the hatter's shop. Dan's father sat out front on the sidewalk in his wheelchair. She couldn't help but smile at the health he exuded since he and Dan started coming for dinner on Wednesday and Saturday.

Now they came every day of the week but Sunday. The elder Waite was a master of persuasion.

"Afternoon." He dipped his head as she approached. "You goin' my way?"

"That I am. After you."

Mr. Waite leaned back and wheeled himself off the edge with practiced skill, and she and Harley followed him across the street with an eye out for hurried automobile drivers.

Dorrie was waiting in a chair on the front porch, but scuttled indoors, through the house, and out the back as Daniel reached the ramp.

Grace drew away toward the barn, then turned Harley and watched the couple from a distance.

They were completely taken up in each other's company and needs, and Dorrie insisted she help him over the threshold in spite of his claim that he could manage himself.

The brief sparring brought to mind her resistance to Dan's help when he prepared her bath.

Her skin warmed at the memory, but it was a pleasurable memory that she refused to view as inappropriate. Dorrie was right. Dan Waite was not most men.

"How did things go today?"

His deep voice behind her no longer caught her unawares. She'd expected him to keep an eye on his father and possibly follow them here. She stepped off Harley and he moved closer, the faint scent of machine oil, leather, and felt about him. He'd been sewing sweatbands.

She was most susceptible to his voice and eyes, both deep enough to draw her in to dangerous waters, and she kept her back to him as she hooked the left stirrup over the horn and loosed the cinch. "I chased a stagecoach up Skyline Drive and down again. Tomorrow, we go out to the ranch to shoot a rescue scene." She lifted the saddle and blanket together, and Dan took them from her and hung them over the hitch rail.

"Would you like to come with us?" She pulled off her thin leather riding gloves a finger at a time, wondering where that had come from. What happened to her "alone" time?

His smile said more than she expected, as if he was encouraged that she'd asked. Then it caved to rationality.

"I still have three hats to finish for Thorson. But next time? I'd like to meet your brothers."

In a taunting mood, she egged him on. "So that's how it is." She slapped the gloves into her open palm. "You finish Thorson's orders before mine and want to meet the infamous Hutton twins, not take a leisurely ride with their sister."

Too late, the implication of her words struck home.

His eyes darkened, and he stepped in even closer.

Caught between his imposing presence and Harley's hulk, her voice sank beyond reach.

With one hand he cupped her braid and slid it through his fingers, his breath heavy with sweet coffee and desire, his eyes drinking her in.

"Your hat." His voice dropped to a raspy depth. "It's finished."

~

Evening chased the sun behind the western ridge, but enough light remained for scrub oak to blush red and aspen to flash their yellow leaves. A complimentary heat flooded Grace's insides as she approached the ranch yard. Merely thinking of her encounter with Dan at the barn sent heat to her cheeks and her heart racing like a runaway stage.

He'd nearly kissed her. She knew it was on his mind, evident each time his eyes dropped to her lips. Confessing her disappointment, even to herself, was a little disconcerting. But what would she have done if he *had* kissed her?

The swing-tree cottonwood stood flat against the graying sky, and a soft light beckoned from the kitchen window. No worry here that anyone would guess she'd come so close to a romantic encounter in spite of swearing them off.

With the quick clap of the screen door, three little cowboys ran her way—cowboys who could ride better than most of the cast.

"Aunt Grace!"

Kip led the bunch in spite of his much shorter stature, and the trio slid to a stop in front of her.

"Are you staying?"

"Can I sit by you at supper?"

"I want to show you my butterfly!"

Jay snorted and Ty shoved Kip to the side. "You don't have no butterfly."

"Do so!" Kip's face reddened and his small hands balled into fists.

"All right, boys. You can't be firing into each other while I'm here, and I'm not here for long."

Three pairs of shoulders slumped, and Kip looked about to cry.

Grace leaned down and braced her hands on her knees. "I can't *wait* to see that butterfly."

A quick wink shot Kip an inch taller and he gave his brothers a snooty glare.

"Be friendly," she told him with a squeeze to his shoulder. "You boys too. Someday your brothers might be the only friends you can count on."

The older two rolled their eyes, just like Hugh and Cale used to. *Boys!*

"Ty, please take care of Harley for me. Jay, will you take my bag inside and tell Helen I'm here for the night? And Kip, please give Helen this little sack, but don't peek."

"I don't gotta peek, I can smell it!"

"And tell her I have news about the movie crew."

"Flickers!" the three cried in unison, loud enough for Harley to lift his head with widened eyes.

Hugh came out of the barn, brushing hay from his shirt and pants.

Grace looked up at the open mow, the grapple fork hanging like an empty jaw. "No wonder you haven't come for the buckboard. Isn't it a little late for making hay?"

He slapped his hat on his leg. "Yup. So where were you when we needed an extra hand?"

"Smart enough to stay in town."

Hugh laughed and scrubbed his hair. "Our third cutting was late this year and we didn't get it over here until yesterday. I'm spreadin' it into the corners."

"I can see that. I wouldn't have minded helping, but I've come today to let you know Selig-Polyscope is on its way up to leave some horses overnight. We're filming a runaway stage on the road tomorrow morning."

He plunked his hat on and folded his arms. "We?"

He couldn't boss her around anymore, but the old challenge sneaked up behind her. She gritted her teeth and matched his stance, arm for arm.

"Yes. And if you want to watch, you're welcome."

He mumbled under his breath and spit off to the side—an inborn characteristic she'd known all her life. But his mumble didn't sound like swear words. Maybe he was making progress.

"I suppose you're doin' the rescuing. You never were much of a damsel in distress."

The snap of his blue eyes let her know he was teasing, but his version of brotherly love still had a bite to it. Maybe Hugh's coarse nature had helped toughen her over the years and set her up to survive Cody's Wild West.

"Cale told those movie folks two years ago that you could outride any fella they had in their crew." He almost looked proud.

"Thank him for me—unless he shows up and I'll thank him myself."

~

It'd been all Dan could do at the barn not to sweep Grace into his arms. The electricity between them still triggered through his veins as he remembered the softness of her hair, its scent. Oh, to loosen that braid and splay his fingers through it …

Reluctantly, he focused on the hats lining his work bench. Nine, to be exact, six of them matching the color, size, and style ordered by Thorson. He stacked them loosely for delivery to the studio. Six cast members had come by in the last couple of days for their final fit and shaping, one a slender fella with black hair and pale eyes that didn't track long on any one thing.

Three blanks remained unformed, and Dan planned to work on them through the evening. He had other business for tomorrow.

He'd left his father in Dorrie's care, which was akin to asking a cat if it wanted cream. If she had downstairs quarters, he'd consider boarding Pop there. It had crossed his mind that both he and Pop could rent rooms, but the stairs concerned him. He didn't think his father could handle them, and he didn't want to find out the hard way.

Plans to finish the screened-in porch bunched up in the back of his mind as he placed the finished hats in a long cotton sack. It wouldn't take much to turn the porch into a legitimate room, maybe add a small parlor stove. The general or hardware store should be able to get one, and he could vent it through an outside wall.

With sack in hand, he locked the doors and set out for the studio.

No crowd of people milled out front this afternoon, and few were inside working on wardrobe and props. Thorson was in his office on the telephone—a luxury Dan wished Dorrie and Grace had at the house.

He studied the painted backdrops against one wall, used for converting the open space into a saloon, parlor, and other settings.

"Waite!" Thorson strode across the room. "Looks like you've got a stack o' hats there."

Dan offered his hand, then the sack. "Six of your cast came by for the final fit and shaping. I've penciled their names inside the crowns. The last three should be finished tonight, but they'll still need to be tried on and shaped."

Thorson set the hats out on a long bar-front toward the back of the room.

Dan turned each one over on its crown. "If you don't set them on their brims, they'll hold their shape better."

"Is that a fact?"

"Yes, sir. Some would also say it keeps the luck from running out, but I don't buy into that."

"You don't?" Thorson picked up a couple of hats and looked inside the crowns. "What *do* you believe in?"

"God and good sense."

Thorson's raucous laugh drew people from doorways along one side of the long room.

The director pulled a roll of money from his pocket and peeled off several bills. "In the name of good sense, here's what I owe you for all nine. I'll send the other three men down this afternoon. We need the hats by tomorrow morning. Can you handle that?"

If he worked all evening and into the night. "I won't be in the shop tomorrow, but I'll leave them at the widow Berkshire's behind the feed store. A two-story white house. You can pick them up there."

Thorson rubbed his chin. "Isn't that where Grace Hutton is staying?"

CHAPTER SIXTEEN

Dan eyed a deep-chested, sorrel gelding at the livery. "I need a good saddle horse for tomorrow. All day."

Smitty quoted his price. "You ridin' out to Hutton's with the flicker crew?"

Not much was confidential in Cañon City, especially when it came to the film company. "Not with them. But can you tell me how to get there?"

The blacksmith's thick mustache spread nearly to his ears. "You're gonna watch Grace rescue that runaway stage."

"Yeah." It wasn't any of the fella's business, but a good horse was. "See if the rumors are true."

"That she can ride, rope, and shoot better than her brothers and every other fella in Fremont County?" Smitty shook his head and wiped his blackened hands on a dirty rag from his back pocket. "She's been doin' that since before she was growed up. Then she went off and made a living at it with that Buffalo Bill outfit. You know, that's what took her away to begin with. That Wild West show stopped here about four years ago, and she was hooked. Her brothers didn't think much of the idea, but that didn't stop her."

No surprise there. "I'll be leaving near sunup."

Smitty stepped out from the hitch rails and looked up Main Street. "Take this road here all the way out of town." Pointing, as if he could see to the end, he added, "When you get to Soda

Point, follow the curve on around the hill and keep goin' past the turnoff that takes you up to Skyline Drive. About a mile after that, there'll be a road that cuts off to the north, just before another big turn to the left. Take that road five or six miles up, and the main ranch road will be on your right. Big gate entrance with a high crossbeam, though you'll already be on Hutton land. All that good cow country up there belongs to them."

Dan paid the blacksmith. "Thank you. I'll be here early."

He didn't know what time Thorson and his crew would get to the ranch, but he'd just as soon get there first, which meant he had work to do.

He checked the traffic and cut across the road to the lane by the feed store. At the boarding house, he stomped his boots off at the front door, knocked on the screen, and at a cheerful "Come in," trailed back to the kitchen.

Pop and Dorrie sat at the table enjoying pie and coffee. Quite a habit for his father to take up at his age. But the fact was, he didn't look his age any more. Somewhere along the way sorrow had sloughed off and taken the fruitless years with it.

"I wondered if you'd be back in time for supper." Dorrie set another plate and cup on the table, then served a generous slice of canned-cherry pie.

Dan hung his hat on the hook by the back door and took a seat. "Thank you, Dorrie. This will do for me. I won't take supper this evening. I've got three hats to finish before tomorrow."

"Why the rush?" Pop asked.

"I'll be gone tomorrow, all day I expect. Which reminds me, Dorrie, would it be all right if—"

"By all means," she said. "I have a dozen crocuses and some hyacinths that arrived last week, and I want to get them in the ground."

"You didn't ask if it was all right with me." Pop cut Dorrie a side glance, then winked at Dan.

Coughing to disguise his amazement, Dan took his plate to the sink. "All right, Pop. What do you think of spending the day here tomorrow?"

"She wants to put me to work in her garden. Thinks I'm closer to the ground than she is."

Pop's sense of humor was sprouting like those bulbs would next spring. "Well, don't work him too hard, Dorrie."

"Pffft." She swatted the air and topped off his father's coffee cup.

Pop nodded his thanks to Dorrie with a tender look, then focused on Dan. "Are those three hats for the film company?"

"Yes, the final three. Thorson paid me, and I told him they'd be ready tomorrow morning. If you don't mind, Dorrie, I said he could pick them up here. I'll leave them in a bag on the front porch so they won't be any trouble to you."

"No trouble at all, dear. You leave all you want out there."

Pop set his mug down. "I'll come over and help you after supper, then bring the hats over with me tomorrow morning."

Dan nearly told his father no, but at the renewed sense of purpose in his eyes, he relented. "Thanks, Pop."

He returned to the shop as three of the moving picture crew showed up for a fitting. Pop joined him an hour later. Working together, they had the hats finished before midnight. Dan was up well before dawn and stacked the three felts in a cotton bag. He could hear his father getting himself together, and Pop soon rolled out to the main room, his hair slicked back and a clean shirt buttoned all the way to the top.

"You look mighty fine for this early in the morning, Pop."

His father wheeled over to the work bench and set the bag in his lap. "I've got hot coffee, fresh bread, and a sweet woman waitin' for me. Darn right I'm fine on this brand-new day. Lock the door behind me."

Instead, Dan followed him outside and checked the street.

"You tell her?"

Facing his inquisitor, who sat arrow straight in his cane-backed chair, Dan confessed, "Yes, sir, I did. And you were right."

A quick nod and Pop leaned back and rolled off the edge of the sidewalk. "Of course I was."

As Dan watched him cross the empty road, turn down the lane, and disappear around the back of the feed store, he felt he was watching an actual miracle unfold right in front of him. This time last month, he would have denied it was possible.

The city awoke around him—automobiles coughing to life, dogs barking in complaint. The faint slap of a screen door told him Pop made it to Dorrie's back porch.

His life was shifting again, changing leads, so to speak.

Good Lord, what am I gonna do now?

He went back inside, remembering a similar question asked a few weeks before, but in a different state of heart. God had answered that prayer in a surprising way, and Dan suspected he hadn't seen the entire answer yet.

Thank you, God, for knowin' what You're doing even when I don't.

He grabbed the poke he'd filled for himself and a rolled slicker, locked the doors, then walked down to the livery. Smitty was at his forge already and the horse was waiting out front at the hitch rail, saddled and ready to go.

"Pascoe'll do right by you," the blacksmith said. "He's a good horse. Let him graze some at the ranch, and make sure he gets water."

Smitty didn't figure him for a horseman, so Dan didn't hold the schooling against him. He tied his slicker behind the saddle and slung the bag of food over the saddle horn. Then he checked the stirrup length, gathered the reins, and stepped up.

Smitty looked impressed. "Not your first trip."

Dan smiled as he reined Pascoe away and into a brisk walk. "Nope."

At Soda Point, he followed the road around the bend and looked back over his shoulder. A thin red line bled along the eastern horizon, and dark clouds banked it down, promising a storm later in the day. He prayed the rain and lightning would hold off until Grace's rescue scene was finished.

The farthest he'd been from town in a year was the Hot Springs Hotel, up river toward the gorge. But the landscape around him now lifted outcroppings of stone on one side, cedar-dotted slopes on the other. More like high dessert, away from the river. Ochre, brown, and near-green layered a bluff-face rising well above the road to the Skyline. He'd not been up that rocky spine, but he'd heard talk of the view it offered.

After passing its west entrance, he kicked Pascoe into an easy lope, watching for the turnoff. The sky brightened by a degree, and soon the dregs of night slipped behind the western mountains.

He wasn't sure what to expect today, other than watching Grace do what he wished she wouldn't. It involved more than her and Harley this time. Too many moving parts with a stagecoach team and driver, other people, and the bulky coach itself.

The farther he rode, the heavier his chest ached with a memory he couldn't shake, but he'd be there if things went south. He'd be there this time—older, stronger. And not alone.

"Lord, help this stubborn woman who's determined to attempt the near impossible. If You don't change her willful mind, please—please protect her."

~

A restless night was no way to prepare for a performance, but Grace had little say in the matter. Anticipation set her blood to racing like it always had before a show.

Dressed in what she wore the day before on the Skyline, she joined Helen and Mary already starting breakfast. Lamp light warmed the kitchen, and fresh coffee called from the stove.

"It smells so good in here. What can I do to help?"

"Morning, Grace." Mary's greeting vied with the welcoming aroma of biscuits and sausage gravy.

"You can set the table." Helen hugged her briefly. "It's nice to have you here, even if it is temporary, though I'm not real pleased with what you shared last night. Land's sake, Gracie, can't they get a man to jump from horseback to a runaway stagecoach?"

The back screen slapped shut. "Nope, 'cause Cale and I aren't signed on this year. Too busy with the fall gathering." Hugh wrapped his arms around Mary and gave her a kiss. "Not that Cale wouldn't have done it anyway. But he's married now, so he's smarter."

Grace caught Mary's eye roll and nearly snorted.

Leaving his wife, Hugh yanked Grace's braid. "You know how he is."

Oh, she knew. The Hutton brothers vied for top billing just like the younger generation vied for seats at the table.

Speaking of the dustups, their stampede flowed through the screen door, proving her point as they pushed and shoved their way to the table.

"Wash!" Grace herself jumped at Helen's command, but the three urchins shot out the back door as quickly as they had come in. Lord, help their school master.

Hugh took his place at the head, and it was clear as day the difference Mary had made in him. She'd softened his rough edges, healed his wounds, and brought a kinder light to his eye. Grace suddenly felt like the odd man out, for she had followed her dream and come home broken and alone.

As they bowed their heads to pray over the hearty meal, Grace wondered again if God could use her mistakes and make things right. She didn't doubt His ability—she knew He could. But she didn't know if He *would.*

Against a youthful trio of "amen," she realized that was the question of her heart.

"Pass the biscuits, please."

As she offered the napkin-lined basket to Kip, who sat across from her, soft as a whisper came the words she'd heard in Grandpa Hutton's study. *Trust Me.*

She glanced at Hugh, then Helen, wondering if they had heard it too. The words had been so sure, so certain, yet apparently inaudible.

Kip opened his biscuit and smeared it with butter. Taking a bigger bite than he should have, he looked Grace right in the eye as he chewed, then gave his head a tight little nod.

As if he knew.

After good food, coffee, and conversation, she helped clear the table but was shooed out of the kitchen with the boys.

"You need time to get ready," Helen said.

True, there was no predicting how long the rescue scene would take today, and she needed to be prepared. She also wanted to see Kip's butterfly.

Outside, across the yard from the house and barn, the stage driver and another fella were readying a team of four. They must have slept in the barn last night, but it would take them a while to get set up, so she called the boys in close.

"Jay, Ty, would you please bring Harley around and brush him down for me?" No sooner had she asked than they were gone, and she turned to Kip. "Get your rope and show me that butterfly."

He dashed to the tack room and returned with the cotton cord, fluttering its loop back and forth.

"Wonderful! You've been practicing, haven't you?"

Proud and beaming ear to ear, Kip stretched to his tallest. "Yes, I have. I want to be a trick roper like you."

"Who told you I was a trick roper?" She squatted beside him and took the cord.

"Why everybody knows it, Aunt Grace."

At least she had something to pass on to the next generation. "All right, then. Here's the next step."

She straightened and set the butterfly wings a-flapping. With a flick of her wrist, she flattened the loop, held it out from her side, and stepped in and out of it.

"Wow!"

"First, you want to get the loop to lie flat, then watch the honda as it comes around next to your leg. You have to step in and out of the loop before the knot comes around again, or it will hit your leg and stop the spin."

She demonstrated again, tapping her toe quickly on the ground, in and out. "It's almost like a dance step, so do it quick."

Kip's face fell and his chin dropped to his chest. "But I can't dance."

"You don't have to," she said. "Just move quickly, as if you *were* dancing."

He tried several times but kept hitting the honda with his leg.

She stooped down next to him again. "It's a hard trick, so don't get discouraged. It took me a long time to learn, but I know you can do it."

She hugged his shoulder. "I have confidence in you."

"What does that mean?"

"I believe in you. That you will work at the trick until you get it, no matter what."

"Harley's all ready." The older boys ran over, brimming with curiosity. "What're you doin' with that rope?"

They moved in on their little brother, their postures demanding an explanation.

Grace waited, aware that a rescue from her would dictate their future treatment of the youngest sibling.

Kip coiled the cord and headed for the tack room. "I'll show you later."

Good job, Kip. Looking heavenward, she offered a silent *thank You.*

Leaving the boys to their chores, she gathered Harley and rode up to what she'd always considered her brother's ridge. Cale used to ride off by himself, unaware that his little sister followed from a distance, curious about why he did such a thing.

These days, she understood. The solitude offered a different perspective on not only the ranch, but life in general.

Cedar branches brushed against her chaps, their blue berries giving off a pungent perfume. Birds skittered—robins and sparrows. A hawk screeched overhead, and from a distance she heard the faint song of a meadowlark.

As she approached the lip of the ridge, Harley's ears cocked forward. He'd never been up on the Hutton heights where a person felt small and insignificant against the legendary Rockies. Ridge after ridge rolled off to the west, but below spread quilted pastures and grazing land, seamed by tree-lined creeks and streams.

Maybe it was age that pushed a person to this ridge, in search of childhood freedom.

It took her breath away—the bird's-eye view that lifted her from care and responsibility. Made her unreachable and immune to worry, fear, and heartache. Alone, yet not—as if seated at the foot of a loving Creator she could … *trust*.

"It's beautiful, isn't it, ol' boy?"

Harley blew and bobbed his head, his ears swiveling from the scene below to Grace's voice.

The sun was long up now, more than an hour, and it peeked over heavy clouds in the east, promising a fight sometime later in the day—a fight between wind and rain and maybe lightning. Depending on when the storm broke, the team on that runaway stagecoach might need no prompting at all.

She stood in her stirrups, catching a breeze that teased hair away from her face. A big part of her wished that Dan had come along. She'd like him to see the ranch from this viewpoint. See the sunrise and smell the coming rain.

But maybe it was best that he hadn't. He was spreading out in her heart the same way the ranch spread out below her.

If he truly had feelings for her, he'd have to make the move on his own, like he had yesterday morning, surprising her with unexpected tenderness. He'd caught her off guard and left her wanting more.

She had to be sure that the "more" was God's doing this time, and not her own longing.

Harley's ears flicked toward a thin dust plume spiraling at the far end of the valley, where the ranch road cut off from the long stretch up Eight-Mile Hill. No automobile, just a lone rider.

She expected the crew and Thorson to arrive any time now. But who would be riding up this way alone and so early?

CHAPTER SEVENTEEN

Dan walked Pascoe across a slow creek with clusters of white-barked, yellow-leafed aspen. Autumn came earlier at this elevation, and the higher he got, the more aspen trickled down the gullies. He could spend a lifetime in this country, taking in the clean mountain air and quiet beauty—until an automobile coughed into his reverie.

He reined off the road and watched a three-car parade approach, stirring up enough dust to choke a bear. Spotting a game trail that climbed away from the road, he followed it up and out of the racket.

No stagecoach team followed. They must have come up the day before.

A quarter mile ahead, two automobiles pulled off to the side and one continued on.

He kept to the trail that paralleled the road and stopped on a knoll with a good view of Thorson, the cameramen, and a handful of actors. The place they'd chosen was rimmed on one side by a rocky outcropping with few trees.

How difficult would this stunt be for Grace? An uncontrolled setting. No arena or grassy park. He took in all angles from the road, noting a clear way down from his vantage point in case things didn't go as planned.

His pulse spiked.

Who in their right mind *planned* a runaway stage?

He'd heard horror stories of wrecks in moving pictures. The more he thought about it, the less he liked it. But he had no say over what Grace did. It'd be like her coming into the shop and telling him how to finish a hat—a task that did not involve broken necks.

He stepped off Pascoe and looped one rein over a cedar branch. Then he took a heel of bread from his sack and settled down to await the show.

Why couldn't Grace be like other women? A homemaker. A teacher or nurse.

He laughed at his own question. She was all those and more. But one thing was for certain—she wasn't like other women. He wouldn't be out here if she was.

An unfamiliar rattle came from up the road, and he stood to see the stage coming his way at an easy pace. Grace followed a ways back on Harley. No dust-eating ride for her.

She wore the hat he'd first seen her in, and he checked the actors to find most of them in the new hats he'd sold Thorson.

As Grace approached, his eye sharpened on her long braid, the way she sat the saddle, as if she'd done this a hundred times. Maybe she had.

But it didn't make it any easier watching her risk her life.

From a distance behind him, a low rumble rolled across the hills. Not a cloud in the blue expanse above him, but over his shoulder a slate-gray bank stretched between sky and rocky earth.

Living a year in Cañon City had taught him how quickly a storm could sweep in over the town. But out here in the open country?

He'd soon know.

~

Grace circled around the stage's choking dust at the same time thunder growled in the distance. They'd better get going or they'd all be caught in a gully-washer.

"Grace—there you are." Thorson approached with megaphone in hand. "I want to get this done on the first take, so look over the stagecoach and horses and talk to Regi—you saw him up at Skyline. He won't be falling off this time—he'll be in an oversized front boot under the seat and out of view, holding the reins. We've got two cameras—one up front and one behind you and the stage. I want you to jump onto the driver's box, pick up the reins, and slow the horses to a stop."

He indicated a woman in Victorian garb with an oversized hat. "Frances here will be hanging out the window on your side, screaming and waving her arms."

Wonderful.

"I take it that's the left side of the stage—away from the rocks—and on my right."

"You got it."

Grace rode back to Regi who was checking bridles and traces. At Skyline, he'd been "shot" and jumped off the stage in what appeared to be a fall.

"Are your reins in good shape?" she asked.

"Yes, ma'am." He gave her a quick once-over. "I hear you rode with Cody's show. They had stage scenes, didn't they?"

"Oh, yes. Runaways, hold-ups—the whole deal."

Regi chuckled. "Then you'll be right at home. Welcome to the flickers."

Wardrobe snagged her for makeup and costume, and the hairdresser jammed at least a dozen hairpins into her scalp to secure her wig-hidden braid and costume hat.

One cameraman took off on foot down the road. The other jumped into a roadster with his equipment, and the driver headed back toward the ranch, then turned the car around to face the stage.

Thorson raised his megaphone. "Places!"

Grateful that Harley was warmed up from the morning's ride, Grace stroked his neck and rode away from the crowd and commotion. "Lord, help us," she prayed in a cooing tone, assuring Harley with her voice that all was well.

His ears swiveled between her voice and the road ahead, and he eased into his ambling gait.

She slowed him to a walk and leaned low over his neck, reins tight in her fingers. "You can do this, Harley. You've run after stages before and this one has only four horses, not six. Get me close, boy. You remember the cues."

In spite of her efforts to smooth out her voice and movements, lather formed on Harley's neck beneath the reins. He was ready but anxious. So much was so different. *Lord, You know our every step. We can't do this without Your help.*

"Ready!" Thorson's amplified voice sounded frail and distant at a hundred yards.

Twenty feet from the roadster, she turned and faced the stagecoach.

They had one chance. One chance to do it right, because if they didn't, either she or Harley would be hurt so badly they couldn't attempt it again.

Lightning hit, drawing Grace's eye to the lowering clouds. In three counts, thunder followed.

Three miles out.

For I know the thoughts that I think toward you … thoughts of peace, and not of evil, to give you an expected end.

An expected end—her expectations or God's? She tightened her hold on Harley's reins as he pranced and blew in anticipation.

"Action!"

Grace leaned forward and slammed her smooth-roweled spurs into Harley with a yell—" "Hyah!"

~

Thunder rolled behind Dan, and Grace's horse leapt into a full gallop.

He'd never seen the likes of it.

The stage lunged forward, riderless reins slapping on the horses' rumps amid hollers from the hidden driver.

An automobile carrying a cameraman followed close behind Grace, and another cameraman stood his ground at the edge of the road a couple hundred yards ahead of them.

Dan jumped up, unable to sit while watching this woman he cared for ride like a wild man, closing ground on what appeared to be a runaway stagecoach.

A garishly dressed actress inside the coach leaned out a window and screamed, waving her arms.

"God, help Grace do this." Dragging his eyes from Harley bearing down on the stage, Dan caught the snap and flail of leather straps as they dropped between the lead pair.

His lungs locked. No one came to the rescue.

Was he the only person who could see that the reins had broken?

Grace caught up to the stage, running dangerously close to it. Preparing to jump from her saddle to the box, she pulled her left foot from the stirrup, but hesitated.

Looking ahead, she kept Harley running, but found her stirrup and spurred him on. The gelding stretched his neck out and lengthened his reach until they were neck and neck with the lead team.

Grace dropped her left stirrup again and leapt onto the near leader's back. Lying along its neck, she reached between the two horses for their bridles and came up with the inside rein on each one.

Dan's heart jammed in his throat.

The horses began to slow, heads up, eyes wide as they passed the photographer, prancing and bouncing to a rattling stop.

"Cut!" Thorson ran for the stagecoach as dust fled from the advancing storm.

Lightning struck close and thunder echoed against the rocks. The lead pair reared in the harness, but Grace held her seat.

Harley pranced at her side, tossing his head.

The stage driver crawled out of the boot and held the broken reins up to cheers and cries from the crowd.

Another thunder clap, and the skies opened, drenching horses, riders, cars, and cameras.

Dan caught Pascoe and raced down the sloping bluff to Grace.

In spite of the downpour, actors and crew had already gathered around her, but he jumped off in their midst, unlashed his slicker, and wrapped it around her shoulders. Then he hauled her off the team leader and set her on Harley. Against the downpour and congratulatory crowd, he yelled, "How far to the ranch?"

She whirled Harley around. "Follow me!"

CHAPTER EIGHTEEN

The storm gathered its skirts and swept away to the high parks and pine forests.

Side by side, Grace and Dan rode beneath the crossbar of the Rafter-H gate. At the barn, they stripped their horses' tack, settled them in stalls, and pitched in hay.

Grace waited in the alleyway, wrapped in yellow oilcloth, while Dan filled water buckets. "Thank you for the slicker. I'd be drenched without it."

Drenched himself, he pulled his hat off and drew her to him, holding her close—protectively, as if she'd fly away. Even the slicker's heavy material failed to hide the pounding of his heart.

She laid her hands against his chest. "You were the solitary rider I saw this morning."

His eyes confirmed her suspicions, then shuttered, hiding something.

"What? What is it?"

Cupping her face with his hand, he took in the wig and her hat. "I miss your braid. Let's get you inside."

She resisted his lead, stood her ground. "What is it, Dan? What's troubling you?"

His jaw tightened, clamping off his words, and his face grew cold. Distant.

She began to tremble. "Why did you ride up here today? You told me you couldn't make it, that you had work to do, hats to finish. Why were you here?"

Deep in her gut she knew something was wrong and it had to do with her. With what she did and the risks she took. They'd talked about it, and she thought the air had cleared between them, but there was more. And he wasn't willing to reveal it.

He grabbed her hand. "Come on, let's get inside. We can talk later."

He took off, forcing her to follow. They splashed like children through puddles catching sunlight and burst through the back door with the finesse of her nephews.

Helen looked up from the stove, her wooden spoon stilled over a pot of something that stirred Grace's belly with hunger. A moment's hesitation then, like a sword, she pointed the spoon at the back wall. "Hang your wet clothes on that rack and get yourself some coffee."

Nothing had ever startled Helen.

Dan took the slicker as Grace slid it from her shoulders and hooked it beside his dripping hat.

She hurried to the stove and hugged the housekeeper's girth. "Helen, I'd like you to meet Dan. The hatter I told you about." Realizing she'd given herself away, she bit her tongue.

"It's a pleasure to meet you, ma'am." No easy smile, just simple respect. "Sorry about our sudden appearance and soaked condition."

"Leave your boots over there too, and I'll get dry socks for you." Helen set aside her spoon and wiped her hands on her apron. "Land's sake, you look like a couple of drowned rats kicked off Noah's ark."

Grace pulled off her wet hat and wig, and Dan hung them on hooks as well. Water dripped intermittently from one item or another, adding a rhythmic sidenote to the room's warmth.

A dozen hairpins piled up as Grace finished unpinning her braid and rubbed her sore scalp. Tanned hides nailed to the barn could not feel worse.

She filled two mugs from the cupboard with hot coffee and sugar and set one across the table from her for Dan.

As he sipped the hot brew, his eyes closed.

"I know," she whispered. "It's amazing, isn't it." Open-eyed, she drank in the strong coffee as well as his masked expression. A splatter of mud had caught his chin, but she held her cup with both hands, fighting the urge to run her fingers over that strong jaw and wipe it clean. If only she could wipe away the mask as well.

Helen bustled in, cementing Grace's self-control. "Here are dry socks for the both of you. Hugh won't miss 'em."

"Thank you, Helen." The woman had always thought of things that other people missed. "I'll get these back to you as soon as I can."

"Will you be staying the night? That was quite a storm we had. Could have washed out the road in places."

"No, we can't. Dan's father and the widow Berkshire are waiting on us. I don't want to leave her alone any longer than necessary." She glanced at Dan.

"And I need to get my father back to his room at the shop."

"Well, you can stay long enough for dinner. The boys, Hugh, and Mary are bringing down cows with Cale. Unless they hunkered under the chuckbox tarp, they're no drier than you two, but I don't expect them back until suppertime."

Grace swallowed her disappointment, but it might be for the best if they wanted to get back before dark. "I'll set the table for you while Dan fills you in on what we did today."

He scoffed. "What we did isn't the story. It's what *Grace* did."

Helen tossed him a worried look. "Do I want to know?"

His comment confused Grace, and she busied herself at the counter lining a basket with napkins and piling in warm biscuits. For years she'd performed before anxious crowds, thrilling them with her daring stunts. But Dan's assessment made her wonder what he really thought.

After dinner, she helped Helen with the dishes and filled a quart jar with stew for Dan's father.

"I'll send some gingersnaps with you too. It's not like I don't have six dozen of 'em." Helen wrapped the jar in a towel and put it in a sack along with the cookies. "Tie this on carefully, and you'll make it back to town with it intact. Hopefully there won't be any more runaway stagecoaches along your way."

She wrapped Grace's wig in another towel and added it to the sack. "You two be careful and come back when you can stay longer. I'm sure the boys will be sad they missed you."

Grace hugged the woman who had done so much for her over the years, then gathered her bag of clothing from the day before and went to saddle Harley.

Dan lingered at the door, attentive to something Helen was telling him.

When he finally showed up, Grace had his horse saddled as well and was waiting by the hitchrail.

"I see you still have both ears."

He stepped up on Pascoe. "You figure she'd talk my ears off tellin' stories on you?"

Grace turned Harley toward the ranch road, heavier of heart than when they'd arrived. "She's got enough to do that very thing."

Thorson and company were long gone from where they'd filmed, and several small gullies cut across the road from the downpour, leaving miniature waterfalls.

Grace's shoulders ached from the day's ordeal. She'd spent too many weeks idle, a condition she'd not known during Cody's shows. But the timing had been perfect for the stunt, thank the Lord, in spite of her last-minute change of plans. That was so like God to be ready for every contingency.

She just hadn't been ready for Dan to show up.

Anxiety crawled in and camped beneath her gratitude, and she cut him a side glance. Ironically, she'd felt no fear while sliding from Harley to the running team. What she dreaded more than physical injury was being made the fool again.

As they rode into town, dusk crept in behind them—that time of day when eyes played tricks and shadows clung beneath the eves of buildings as if looking for shelter. Lights warmed windows at the Denton Hotel and in upstairs rooms above several stores along the muddy Main Street. She imagined people settling in for the night, fixing supper, relaxing with those they loved. She was not so naïve as to believe every human situation was idyllic, but she'd often dreamed of such a setting in her own life.

Nights on the road with Cody's Wild West Show offered no such comfort, but lately it had taken little effort to imagine creating a homey atmosphere with Dan. Now, maybe not.

At the livery, she waited out front while he returned his horse, then walked across the street with him to Dorrie's. A welcoming light filled the parlor windows and spread through the house to the kitchen as well. Maybe this was as close to home as she'd ever get.

"You go on in and I'll see to Harley." With the reins under her arm, she untied the sack. "Give this to Dorrie as a peace offering since we're so late. But remember, the stew is for your father."

Again, those eyes, still dark. Still deep, but cold. Lightless.

"Don't be long."

No brushing aside her hair this time. No lingering touch. She couldn't read his words. Command or request? Careless or concerned.

Her struggle knocked every reasonable thought from her mind, and as he walked away, she tried to remember why she was standing there holding Harley's reins in the dark.

~

A sense of relief hit Dan as he entered the kitchen, but it wasn't his own.

Dorrie shot up. "I'm so glad you're back."

His father gripped the sides of his chair as if to stand himself.

The hair on Dan's neck raised. "What is it?"

At the door glass, Dorrie peered into the dark. "Grace is with you, isn't she?"

"Yes. She's tending to Harley." He set the bag on the table and gently took Dorrie by the elbow, guiding her back to her chair. "What's wrong? Did something happen while we were gone?"

His father's sigh expelled a day's worth of tension, and he slumped against his chair's cane back. "We've been a little on edge, is all. And then when you didn't return before sunset, we began to worry."

Dorrie pushed against the table to stand, but Dan touched her shoulder. "I'll get it. What do you need?"

"It's what *you* need—coffee."

"I'll get it. You rest."

"I've been resting all day and I'm jittery as a worm in spring."

Pop reached for her hand and took it in both of his, understanding and compassion filling his eyes and gentling his tone. "Let him get it, Dorrie."

The warmth in his father's voice poked a spot beneath Dan's vest that was already sore. Never had he thought he'd hear such an emotion from his father again. Everything had died inside the man when he lost his wife.

This evening, that warmth sounded a lot like hope.

Dan added coffee and water to the pot, pulled it over the front burner, and stoked the fire.

If Grace didn't get there in the next two minutes, he was going out to—

"Sorry we're so late." The door closed softly behind her, and she pulled off her soppy hat and hung it on a hook. "Maybe this is why fall is known as fall. It's the sun, not the leaves, that drops so fast, you hardly get anything done."

When no one said a word, she glanced around the table. "What is it?"

Dorrie's hand was still in Pop's. "You tell her, Daniel."

"We had a visitor this morning, a young fella who came to get the hats Dan left here."

Dan's attention sharpened. "Did he give you any trouble?"

Dorrie shuddered. "What he gave me was the willies."

"Why is that?" Grace dropped into the chair next to her.

"He was real shifty-eyed," Pop said. "Nervous. Couldn't keep his focus on any one thing. And he had unnaturally black hair—one of those flicker folks, for sure."

Dan leaned in. "Did he cause trouble? Was he rude?"

Dorrie's face paled, and she looked at Grace. "I think he was the boarder who robbed me."

"The one who hit you?" Grace said. "And knocked you down?"

Pop tugged Dorrie's hand closer. "You didn't tell me he robbed you. Why didn't you say something?"

She inched her chair toward his. "And have you challenge him?"

Grace rubbed her forehead, her eyes squinty as she glanced at Dan and back to Dorrie. "Oglethorpe, you said his name was. Didn't he have long fair hair and a mustache like Bill Cody?"

"Yes," Dorrie said. "But this fella had the same pale eyes, slight build, and jerky movements. I think it was him. I was worried all day that he'd come back."

Dan set his cup down hard and pushed back from the table. "We're all staying here tonight. Pop, I'll set you up in the parlor. I'll take the porch room. You women are upstairs."

He focused on Dorrie. "Do you have a gun?"

Gray eyes hardened like polished steel. "It's been a while since I've used it, but Henry's shotgun is in the study."

"Grace," he said, turning to face her. "I hear you're a crack shot. Do you have a firearm with you?"

CHAPTER NINETEEN

Regret had always snake-bit Grace at inappropriate times, and this one was as untimely as ever. Why hadn't she thought to bring one of the rifles from the ranch? At least a handgun.

"No, I do not."

"Doesn't matter." Dan stepped behind her and his strong hands gently squeezed her shoulders, reassuring her. "I'll bring what I've got at the shop."

His words were as close to a charging bugle call as anything she'd heard. The only part of his plan she didn't like was him sleeping on the porch.

"Your father can sleep in the study—I'll show you where it is—and you can sleep in the parlor. You won't fit on the settee, but I'll make a pallet for you."

Dorrie stood and smoothed her apron. Calmer now, she addressed Daniel. "You can help me bring all the lamps to the kitchen and fill them. I'll gather some from the upstairs rooms that aren't being used, and we'll set them around down here."

Grace went to the wood box by the stove and picked up the burlap carrier. "I'll bring in kindling for the stove and wood for the parlor in case it cools off tonight."

As Dorrie and Daniel headed to the front of the house, Grace moved close to Dan. "Do you want me to go with you to the shop?"

Amusement tainted his smile, but he was wise enough not to mock her. "I'd rather you stayed here with Dorrie and Pop—

in case they need you." He brushed aside her mussed hair. "I won't be long."

After the door closed, Grace dropped the carrier and ran to the front of the house, where she watched from the parlor window as Dan faded into a shadow. Cañon City's street lights did little to illuminate storefronts with awnings, and her eyes strained to see the hat shop window and recessed doorway.

She stared unblinking, unaware she wasn't breathing until he reappeared. Her first breath shot pain from one side of her head to the other and made her eyes ache.

At the sound of his boot on the bottom porch step, she opened the front door, then quickly closed it behind him and turned the key.

He wore a sidearm that must have been his father's, an old Colt .45.

Oglethorpe best think twice about coming back to the boarding house under cover of dark.

~

A hidden room was the last thing Dan expected when Grace slid aside a paneled partition beneath the stairs. She set a lamp atop a large cherrywood desk and turned up the wick. The long narrow room spoke of a man and his books—her preacher grandfather. At the opposite end stood a daybed with a chair and small end table.

Grace lit another lamp already there, and the room brightened even more. She was right.

"This is perfect, Grace."

She smiled but kept her eyes from his.

He knew she felt cut off, like something had jammed in between them, but now wasn't the time to be thinking of anything but Dorrie and Pop's safety. And Grace's.

"I'll run upstairs for blankets and make a pallet for you in the parlor."

As soon as she left, he spotted the shotgun in the corner. Suspecting shells had been kept in a bottom desk drawer, he checked and found them on the first try, then took them and the gun to the kitchen.

Unwilling to let Grace bring in firewood, he did so while she gathered bedding. With his holstered .45, his hands were free to hold the burlap carrier full of kindling as well as an armload for the parlor fireplace. He left the kindling in the kitchen and stacked wood on the parlor hearth before bringing in a second armload and locking the back door.

When she came down the stairs with blankets and quilts stacked to her chin, a fire was crackling in the parlor.

"Oh, I forgot about the wood. Thank you." She set her burden on a chair and rolled out a wool blanket and a couple of quilts. Folding each into three long layers, she wrapped them all with a sheet and tucked it in around the edges like an envelope, as near to a canvas bedroll as he'd seen in a long time. No one had gone to such trouble for him since his ma. He certainly didn't.

She topped it all with another quilt but traded it for one that had squares of faded red stars.

Attempting to penetrate the barrier between them, he asked, "Is that one warmer than the first one you had?"

Still sober, she patted a star. "I like it more, that's all."

He knelt beside her as she tucked it in around the edges, refusing to meet his eyes. If he wanted to—

"This is the quilt my grandmother gave to my grandfather when he was sleeping in a stall at the livery."

That was the last thing Dan expected to hear.

"My father was their first child—Whit, named after Grandmother's father, Daniel Whitak—"

The name caught Grace's breath, and he watched her try to hide her surprise.

"Daniel Whitaker," he said, keeping his voice low and easy. *Daniel.* "D.W."

Hands folded tightly in her lap now, Grace lowered her head. "I hadn't thought of that."

The story intrigued Dan as much as watching Grace's face betray her emotions. What would it be like spending evenings—and days and mornings and nights—with a woman like this, so full of life?

Again, risk. It'd be a risk telling her. She might hate him. Think him a coward or incompetent. Why was it that what he dreaded most kept popping up in front of him?

"Here are two more lamps for the parlor." Dorrie's spry voice broke through the intimacy of their conversation as she and Pop entered. Dan warred with the idea of ushering the widow out of her own parlor so he could be alone with Grace.

Instead, he stood. "I'll take that for you."

"What a lovely fire you have going here, Dan. Please put that lamp on the mantel."

Grace scrambled to her feet, brushing off the denims she'd worn since the stagecoach rescue.

"Daniel, will you please set your lamp on the table by the settee?"

Dan caught Grace's eye, noting her discomfort. Was it the stiff clothing she wore? Or did she think it foretelling that Pop shared the same name as her great-grandfather?

~

Well after midnight, Grace still couldn't sleep, though she checked at regular intervals to make certain Dorrie did.

Daniel Waite had been quite pleased with his quarters in the study and even commented on the "smell of the place."

She and Dan exchanged a conspiratorial glance at his father's obvious approval of the temporary quarters, which piqued Grace's curiosity about the men's living conditions in their storeroom.

After the awkward moment earlier by the fire, when Dan pointed out the DW connection, she'd not wanted to spend any more time with him that evening—in spite of his unkept promise to talk about what was bothering him at the ranch. She needed distance. A chance to clear her thoughts, and the DW incident merely muddled them. She refused to consider it portentous.

All was still. No movement, no sound, only the mantle clock faintly counting the minutes in the parlor. Night's cloak hung dark and heavy beyond the windows, and separated from him now, she felt unsettled.

Alone in the kitchen, freshening the coffee, she found that she missed him.

"You must be uncomfortable."

Caught off guard by his unexpected presence, she tensed at his ability to read her thoughts. She had always prided herself on keeping her emotions close, unavailable for others to observe.

He leaned against the counter. "I know it's not my place, but you've worn those clothes all day and night, from dry to soaking wet, to dry again."

Relieved by her misjudgment, she glanced over her shoulder to see if he was leering at her or mocking her. Neither. Sincere concern edged his weary eyes.

"You could say the same for yourself, you know."

He took two mugs from the cupboard and held one out. "True."

"I suspect it wasn't your usual, run-o'-the-mill day." She filled his mug, one for herself, and set Helen's gingersnap cookies on the table. Sitting in kitchen chairs eating cookies felt less intimate than sitting on the parlor floor talking about her grandmother's star quilt.

"About that."

That?

He turned his chair and straddled it, angled more toward the cookstove than her. It entertained his eyes, she guessed, gave him something to look at besides her, and she wilted a little on the inside. Three years of riding the rails as well as Harley and other show horses in dusty arenas hadn't exactly made her a raving beauty.

He sipped his coffee, held it with both hands, arms on the chair back, and talked to the stove.

"Our farm was different from your ranch."

Quietly he spoke, as if retelling a memory.

"We lived on the outskirts of Denver—grazing land, horses, a couple cows and their calves. Near the Platte."

She was familiar with the Platte, named by French trappers for its meandering, "braided" waterways and shallow depths.

"My best friend's family lived across the river, and sometimes we'd ride out in the evenings..."

His voice sank, words trailing off. The story unspooled in his eyes, now distant, seeing the story Grace could only hear.

"One fall, we were out, not far from my house. Jimmy had just turned for home when he flushed a bunch of pheasants. They spooked his horse, and it reared, unseating him. Then it shot off across the sand bars."

Grace held her breath, waiting for what she didn't want to hear.

Dan looked into his mug, dropped his voice into its dregs. "Jimmy's foot hung in the stirrup and he screamed for my help."

His words choked off and his hands gripped the mug as if to break it. Even in profile, Grace saw the pain ripping through him.

"I rode hard, but I couldn't catch him. When we reached the barn, Jimmy wasn't screaming anymore."

Grace squeezed her eyes shut.

Dan's ragged breath cut through her as if she were the rescuer who could not rescue, and she looked at him, his jaw muscle clenched and the veins in his neck bulging.

"I couldn't save him. I was there, and I couldn't save him."

Grace wanted to hold this man, comfort him, but he was as tight and hard as the cook stove itself. She laid her hand on his arm, a band of hot iron beneath her fingers.

"Jimmy's pa carried him to the house, came back with his rifle, and dropped the horse where it stood."

Grace could no longer distinguish between heartache and bile, and she fought to swallow both before asking, "How old were you?"

She shouldn't have asked. It didn't matter, but she didn't know what else to say.

"Ten."

Unable to resist, she knelt at his chair and wrapped her arms around him.

With one arm he enclosed her, pulled her near. This gentle man whose hands impacted everything he touched.

No wonder he didn't like what she did—taking chances, making risky rides on horseback. *The Cossack Death Drag. Oh, Lord.*

But it was who she was.

She couldn't be anyone else but herself.

CHAPTER TWENTY

"What do you charge for room and board?"

The previous word had been *amen*, and Dan had risen to get the heated syrup. Halfway there, he stopped and looked at his father.

So did Grace. And Dorrie, who cleared her throat and placed her napkin in her lap but failed to beat Grace to the mark.

"Male or female?" she asked pleasantly. "Pass the hotcakes, please."

Eyes shifted her way.

"Male. Of course, I won't speak for my son, but last night was the best night's rest I've had in years." He liberally buttered his cake and waited for Dan to bring the syrup.

"Pop—"

"The way I see it, I can stay in the back of the hat shop and freeze this winter, or I can rest comfortably in the study." He tipped the pitcher over a stack of warm rounds. "Not to mention, eat considerably better. No offense, son."

And obviously no clue that Dan had cooked this morning. Going to bed at daybreak hadn't made a whole lotta sense, so he stirred up some batter and fried the bacon.

And he should have seen this coming. If he was honest with himself, his father's reasoning made all the sense in the world, except for one thing.

"Dorrie and I will discuss the cost and let you know," Grace said between bites. "But I'm certain an agreement can be reached."

Dan huffed. That was the one thing—cost. He was caring for his father—whose health had improved considerably—and trying to keep a business going. How would he afford room and board as well?

Digging into his own breakfast, he ate slowly, focusing on the tablecloth directly in front of his plate.

"I'm going to the studio this morning. May I stop by for my hat?"

He looked up into clear green eyes. "Sure."

Her expression held no disgust. No judgment for what he'd shared last night. No disappointment. It merely disarmed him in a way he'd not expected. As if he'd expected anything that had happened in the last month.

"It's ready. But I need to adjust the brim to your liking."

"And what about you, Dan?" Dorrie jumped right over the change in subject. "If you were to wall in the porch room and add a small parlor stove, the cost of materials would serve as your rent."

Dan picked up his coffee, stalling. Could he afford the time, materials, and labor for her offer and keep the hat business running at a profitable pace?

"I'll work the numbers and let you know. But thank you for your offer."

Dorrie seemed satisfied with his answer and rose to clear the table.

Grace reached for Dan's empty plate. "I'm going to check on Harley, then I'll be by the shop."

Her smile warmed him from the inside out.

~

Harley held his head a bit lower this morning, and Grace's pulse quickened. His legs were stocked up. She climbed into the corral, cooing under her breath, and rubbing his shoulder. Gently squeezing his left front leg, her fingers left impressions like thumb prints in bread dough.

"I'm sorry, old man. I should have taken you down to the river last night, though trying it in the dark might not have been a good idea. Let's give it a go now."

She haltered him and led him along the path through underbrush to the river. The memory of Oglethorpe making his getaway here sent a shiver up her spine. Had the sheriff had any success finding the scoundrel? Had he even tried?

Or was Oglethorpe right under his nose, working for the filming company?

"Hold on, boy, while I take off my boots and stockings."

Harley nosed the flowing water as Grace tucked up the edge of her riding skirt, and together they gingerly stepped into the easy current. So late in the year, the Arkansas ran slower—calm and shallow in places—but still as cold as ever, which was what Harley needed this morning.

He stood contentedly, seeming to enjoy the numbing of his legs. His occasional step splashed rogue waves against Grace's legs, and she in turn scooped the water higher on his.

Removed from the noise of Main Street and tucked behind the trees along the bank, Grace felt as if time slipped away as surely as the water flowed. How mysterious the streaming of both. What memories could the river share if it spoke with human words? It was the very same river that her grandparents had known, yet not the same at all. For the water flowed fresh, always different as it descended from its high headwaters.

Harley dipped his nose and jerked up at its cold kiss, splashing Grace as he did so.

Laughing at his surprise, she tugged his lead. "Come on, you Wonder Horse. We've had enough for one morning. I'll check on you later this afternoon. We may return for a dip just for the fun of it."

Harley lipped grass along the banks while Grace pulled on her stockings and boots with an occasional glance over her shoulder.

Her senses told her things were not as they should be where Oglethorpe was concerned. Perhaps she needed to visit the sheriff again.

However, all she could focus on at the moment was securing Harley in the pasture and stopping by the hat shop.

On her way through the kitchen, she found Dorrie and Daniel playing checkers at the table. "I'm off to the studio and don't know when I'll return. Is there anything I can bring you from town?"

Both seemed intent on their next move until Grace touched Dorrie lightly on her shoulder.

"Oh, no, dear, I believe we have everything we need for a day or so. Though, come to think of it, would you mind stopping by the dry goods store to check their sheeting? Some of our beds could use fresh linens."

One bed in particular, Grace refrained from saying. "I'd be happy to."

"Do we still have any Oreo Biscuits left?" Daniel asked.

We?

Daniel jumped one of Dorrie's pieces and snatched it from the board with the spite of a twelve-year-old.

Dorrie looked aghast.

Grace choked back her laughter and announced on her way to the stairs, "I'll pick up some on my way home."

Her dressing table mirror was less than encouraging, but she did her best with tepid water at the washstand. Plumbing the house with running water would be extravagant, but she could pay for it herself if she stayed.

If she stayed?

As a boarder, of course. If things worked out that way.

She took a brush to her hair, tugging against the knots and digging into her scalp. What was she thinking? This was Dorrie Berkshire's home now, not merely her grandparents' parsonage, and it had been that way for years.

As fresh and together as she could manage, she went out through the front door, reveling in the crisp air and blue sky. Indian Summer for sure. In spite of living so close to town, she knew mere blocks separated the boarding house from the rising bluffs and hills of the area. And with the lengthening evenings, gold had trickled down from the mountains and found purchase in cottonwoods along the river and on scattered street corners here and there.

She had always thrilled at the colors and changes of fall, even as a child. Surely it was the season that set her blood surging rather than the gold lettering on the store window ahead.

As she drew near, she ached for Dan. Would he ever see that his friend's death was not his fault? He'd been a child. Like her nephews. Even they could not have made such a rescue.

And what of herself? Would she ever let go of feeling she'd never measure up?

~

When Dan changed into his last clean shirt at the shop, he realized he needed to visit the laundry as well as the bath house. He and Pop hadn't taken the waters in ages, which meant they both had missed their weekly ritual and could benefit from a regular bath. Dorrie and Grace might send them to the river with a soap cake if they didn't improve their condition and quick.

He looked at the cot where he'd been sleeping for a year next to his father's bed. The room was stuffy and smelled of old sheets and illness. The close quarters weren't the best for Pop, and the last twelve hours at the widow's drove that point home clearer than a spring rain.

But he wasn't so sure he could stay at the boarding house, considering his growing affection for Grace. Not that he didn't trust himself, but the tension might be more than he could handle honorably. Yet as hard as it was to imagine the four of them living under the same roof, it was harder to imagine the rest of his life without Grace.

Something had to be done about it. He could no more live without her than he could walk on top of the Arkansas River. The thought set him back on his heels.

He needed to find out how she felt. He was fairly certain she cared for him, but how much? Enough to marry him? A ragged breath escaped as he came around the curtain into the store front. Marriage would change more than Grace's last name.

Running both hands through his hair, he stopped at a soft click and turned toward the door.

"Good morning."

Gentle. Warm. Not a loud greeting early in the day, as the Good Book warned against.

Grace-filled.

"Good morning." He wanted to ask her right then and there if she'd marry him, but that line shouldn't follow so close on the heels of the first thing a man said to start his day.

"You look …"

Her liquid laughter interrupted. "Like I've been in the river?"

"No. I mean—wait, have you?" He was tripping over his tongue.

She approached the counter in front of the finished hats, looking for hers, he assumed. "I took Harley down this morning. He was stocked up from yesterday's exertion and my neglect. I should have taken him when we got home."

He pulled his stool around from the back of the counter and offered it to her. "Sit here and I'll get your hat."

After a day and night alone with Grace, he shouldn't be nervous. But he was. All thumbs, knees, and elbows. As if he was a fourteen-year-old barely shaving.

He was twice that.

How old was Grace? He lifted the cloth that covered her hat where he'd set it out of sight and reach of other customers.

Old enough to look after herself, that was for danged sure.

He blew away dust that wasn't there and ran his fingers over the crown. Did it matter how old she was? He felt they fit each other, with maybe a few years difference. She couldn't be older based on the fact that she was her brothers' younger sister.

"Dan?"

Blast it. He shut down his daydreaming, came around the counter, and offered the hat.

She stared, unmoving.

Unreasonable fear cinched his chest. Did she not like it? Was it the wrong color, the wrong style?

He pulled deep for a breath.

"Oh, Dan." Her fingers brushed the brim as if it were made of spun glass.

"It won't break—try it on. I'll set out the mirror." His hats could take a beating and still serve the wearer. He prided himself in their durability as well as their style.

Donning it, she looked in the countertop mirror, turning her head first to one side and then the other. She raised her chin and lowered it. And then her beautiful eyes found his. "Would you be offended if I said it was beautiful?"

"No." He leaned in. "And that's definitely the word—beautiful."

She blushed, eyes downcast, nothing like her demeanor the first time she'd come to his shop. "How much do I owe you?" Hopping off the stool, she pulled out her coin purse.

Marry me, Grace Hutton, and I'll cover you for the rest of your life.

Afraid he might say as much, he reached under the counter for his receipt book. "You gave me a dollar. Let's make it an even ten." He'd not charge her what it was worth, but neither would he insult her by not charging her at all.

Tipping her head to the side, she shot him a daring look from beneath the brim. "I know better than that, Dan Waite."

She slid her hand across the counter and a smile across her lips. "You are an artist and a gentleman. But do not be late for supper this evening. And you might want to bring your father's things along. I doubt he'll leave the widow's now for any reason other than to help you occasionally with your hat orders."

In one fluid movement, she stepped back from the counter, lifted her palm, and turned for the door.

Unable to take his eyes off her, he watched until she walked past the window wearing his crowning creation. Only then did he glance at the countertop. Shining against the glass lay a twenty-dollar gold piece.

CHAPTER TWENTY-ONE

Heads turned when Grace walked through the studio door.

Performing in Cody's Wild West Show had conditioned her against the gaping public, those who were sincerely amazed and those who merely gawked. This morning, she attributed such bold appraisal to wonderment over yesterday's stunt with the stagecoach.

Or the hat.

She knew the quality of Dan's work, and had seen enough hats in her travels to know this one was pure beaver with hours of specialized handling. How had he known the exact shape that would fit her, please her? Make her feel …

Cherished.

"Just the person I needed to see." Thorson strode across the room, studying the hat as he did so. He halted in front of her, eyes on the crown. "I'll wager Dan Waite made that hat for you."

Envy curled his lip on one side.

"Yes, sir."

"A lot fancier than the toppers he made for my cast and crew."

"Did he give you what you ordered?" She'd not back away from his veiled accusation.

Thorson cleared his throat and ran a hand over his mouth. "Well, yes. Yes, he did." Rallying, he waved over someone from the back of the room. "But that's not why I wanted to see you. I have a scene in mind and I'd like you to take a look at the area before we shoot it. You didn't happen to ride that horse of yours down here, did you?"

"No, I walked. He needs a rest after yesterday's hard run."

"Yes, yes, well, I can understand that. But I have someone who can take you out to the location."

He held out a hand in introduction. "Miss Hutton, this is Mr. Thorpe. Thorpe, Miss Hutton. I'd like you to take her out to Prospect Heights today so she can check out the situation."

Addressing Grace, he continued, "It's a jail break scene and a swift getaway over rough terrain."

Thorson droned on, but Grace heard little of what he said. Her eyes were locked on the spectacled face of Mr. Thorpe—*Ogle*thorpe. Dorrie had been right.

Chilled by the man's greedy expression, she backed away. She had threatened him weeks earlier from atop Harley. Now she faced him on level ground.

"I haven't the time to make such a trip today," she said. "I have other commitments and must get back to those waiting for me." Two steps took her closer to the door.

"It won't take an hour," Thorson insisted. "I want you to see the area, and Thorpe here has nothing of more importance to do."

Thorpe's expression soured and he cast a snarl behind Thorson's back as he moved closer to Grace. Taking her by the elbow with a smile, a faint click followed, and a sharp prick penetrated her sleeve.

"Ow!" She jerked her arm but couldn't break his grasp. "You're hurt—"

He squeezed tighter and raised his voice. "No trouble at all, Mr. Thorson. I'll be happy to escort Miss Hutton."

Grace twisted her arm to break his hold when someone called Thorson's name, diverting the director's attention.

Thorpe's fingers dug in like claws and he leaned close, his breath vile and sour. "I know where you sleep. I've watched you in the night on the screen porch. When you thought no one was there. And poor Mrs. Berkshire. So trusting in her room upstairs." He pressed closer, his lips on her ear. "First door on the left."

Grace's blood chilled at the graveled words. The sharp point cut deeper into her elbow.

"If you will allow me, I'll get the door for you." He smiled, revealing yellow teeth. "And don't think you can run."

Again close and foul-smelling. "I'll sever your arm as well as your spleen before you can yell for help."

The point pressed deeper and warmth seeped over her skin and ran down her arm. *Blood.*

At the first automobile, he pushed her around to the passenger side, opened the door, and pulled a handkerchief from his pocket that he pressed against her nose and mouth.

Unable to breathe, she bit into his hand, earning a deeper plunge of pain in her left elbow.

Reflexively, she gasped, sucking in what she recognized as chloroform—enough to leave her weak and drowsy. Against her will, she fell onto the seat face first, and he pushed her farther in and closed the door.

Oh, God, help me …

Too soon, they bounced up and over hills, and Grace's insides threatened to revolt. If she could push herself up, she'd empty her stomach in his lap. But her arms had no strength. *Lord, please … send Harley … send Dan, send …*

"Think you're special with that fancy horse, don't you. Well, he's not long for this world. A little loco weed tossed in his feed. Water hemlock, or larkspur will do the trick."

They came to a jolting stop and she rolled onto the floor. If she could just move …

Rough hands grasped her by the arms and dragged her from the car.

"We're in luck." The graveled voice was at her ear again. "The jail is empty today. We won't need it for long, and I happen to know there are two cozy cells in the back."

Her head lolled back and a swath of blue sky passed as her boots dragged across the ground. The squeak of iron, and the sky disappeared, replaced by shadow and the smell of cold stone and dirt. Was she being buried alive?

"They'll catch … you … you'll rot in prison."

"I'll be gone before they notice you're missing. And they'd never think to look for you here."

~

Dan's concentration drained away with the afternoon. He wasn't given to premonitions, but unease gnawed at his stomach. Grace hadn't ridden Harley to the studio, so it would take longer for her to get there and back. But without him, she wouldn't be filming any scenes.

She hadn't passed by the store. What else would keep her away so long?

He pulled out a rag and started wiping down the counter. Maybe she stopped by the grocery. Maybe she went straight home to Dorrie's.

Each click of the minute hand on the wall clock marked a bite on his insides. Hang it all, he was getting nowhere. He tossed the rag, locked both doors, and ran to the boarding house, where he burst through the front door.

Pop was napping in his chair in the parlor and Dorrie looked up from her knitting. "What in heaven's name?"

"Is Grace here?" Calm wasn't at his disposal. "I haven't seen her in three hours. Is she here?"

Dorrie clutched her collar. "You nearly scared the living daylights out of me!"

Picking up her needles, she shook her head. "I dropped a stitch. You sound like a man in—well, a man smitten. Wasn't she going to the studio?"

Dorrie glanced at Pop, who was snoring through the conversation.

"She also planned to stop by the grocery for some Oreo Biscuits. Daniel loves them, you know. I'm sure she's fine."

"I'm *not* sure, Dorrie. I'm going after her."

"Wait—*what*?"

Dan slammed out the back door on his way to the barn.

Harley was wearing out a path along the pasture fence. Upon seeing Dan, he raised his head and whinnied.

"You and me both." Dan took hold of Harley's halter and led him inside, where he exchanged halter for bridle, threw the saddle on, and stepped up. "We're gonna find her."

They walked to Main Street, continued a block west, then turned down a crossroad and took to an alley behind the stores. Watching for foot traffic, Dan hoped to see someone matching his father's description of the fella who picked up the hats. If Dorrie was right, and it was the same fella who attacked her, then Thorson had a hoodlum working for him.

Dan's tension transferred to Harley, and the gelding moved into a running-walk, smoother than a trot and faster as well. Dan gave the horse his head but held him back from a gallop. He'd never ridden a gaited horse before.

"She's all right, Harley." Dan held tighter to that belief than he did the reins. "We'll find her."

They moved swiftly along the alley, and at Third Street, turned for the studio. Dan wrapped the reins around an old hitching post and raced inside.

"Thorson!"

His voice reverberated through the high-ceilinged room and turned heads in his direction. "Where's Thorson?" he yelled louder.

"What's the meaning of this?" The director marched toward Dan, a scowl on his face.

"Where's Grace?"

"Hold on a minute. You can't barge in here and—"

"I just did, and I'll tear this place apart looking for her if you don't tell me where she is," he said. "Now."

Thorson pulled at his collar and glanced around the room.

"Thorpe," someone offered from the side.

"Yes. That's it. She's with Thorpe. He drove her out to Prospect Heights where we plan to film a—"

"Is he a slight fella with black hair and pale eyes?"

Thorson looked worried. "Yes, why?"

Dan grabbed him by his shirt and jerked him close enough to hear his teeth rattle. "If one hair is out of place when I find her, I will hold you responsible."

He shoved the director away and Thorson stumbled back, pulling at his shirt front.

Dan knew where Prospect Heights was and he knew what went on there.

If Oglethorpe hurt her, he'd kill him.

The gelding had worked up a lather on his neck, and Dan grabbed the reins. "Easy, Harley. Don't wear yourself out. We may need all you've got." He mounted and turned back toward Fourth Street and the bridge that crossed the river.

Many a miner wet his whistle in Prospect Heights at the end of a hard day. Saloons weren't all the township had to offer, but Dan refused to consider a worst-case scenario.

"Lord, I need Your help—daylight's leaving me." Harley's ears swiveled back at his voice as if in agreement. "Help me see where she is."

Thorson said they'd driven, but what? Nearly everyone drove nowadays, and Dan wracked his brain to remember what the film crew had driven out to the stagecoach. They were dark automobiles. Roadsters. Not black, but … green. That was it.

He continued down Fourth Street and at a jog in the road, locked on the cut-stone jail house off to the right. His heart sank at the absence of any sort of conveyance. Until he got to the other side of the building.

A dark green roadster sat on the south side of the compact structure.

He dismounted and dropped Harley's reins over the passenger door. "We may need a quick get-away, but I'm sure we'll need a ride home."

Dan eased around to the front of the building, no more than twenty feet wide. A dim light shone through the barred window and a transom above the door. An oil lamp, he guessed, seeing no wires connected to the building. He squatted low and removed his hat, straining to hear through the window.

Someone was talking and it wasn't Grace.

A chair or other object slammed against a wall, and Dan flinched. Sucking a deep breath in exchange for a prayer, he pushed up until he could see through the dirty glass. A dark-haired man stood behind a desk, facing someone in a cell at the back of the building.

Grace.

Anger rose in Dan's throat and his hands clenched. He crawled to the door, grabbed the knob, and slowly turned. Surprise was what he needed. It would be his only weapon.

He crashed in and dove across the desk for Oglethorpe.

"He has a knife!"

In tandem with Grace's cry, Oglethorpe flicked his left wrist back and a blade appeared.

Dan half-crouched and spread his hands wide, no room to circle. Out-armed, he waited for the kidnapper to make the first move.

Wild-eyed, the man lunged, leading with the knife.

The blade caught the flap of Dan's vest.

He grabbed Oglethorpe's arm and slammed his wrist against the desk, disabling the mechanism.

The knife blade fell to the floor, and Dan kicked it toward the cell.

Oglethorpe swung.

Dan ducked and caught him under the chin.

The thug stumbled backward, fell out the door, and landed on his back, unmoving.

"Dan." Grace gripped the cell bars, tears washing her face.

He found the key in a desk drawer, opened the cell, and caught her in his arms.

"I'm never letting you go, Grace. You have to know that—I'm never letting you go."

She wept against his chest until a cry from outside jerked her up.

With his arm at her waist, they approached the open door.

"Hel-help!"

Harley reared and screamed like a war horse, pawing the air and landing inches from a scrambling, shrieking Oglethorpe dragging himself backwards on his elbows.

"Call him off—call him off!"

A small crowd of onlookers had gathered, apparently from surrounding homes and saloons, some laughing and others aghast.

"Call your horse off, mister." A bar tender motioned with his shotgun.

"He's not my horse, but he's defending this woman here who was kidnapped by that squirming weasel on the ground."

"Kidnapped?" The bartender passed his gun to a fella next to him, followed by his towel apron, and waved over two men. "Harold—Otis—help me get this cayuse in the jail. That's what it's for, ain't it? He looks mighty drunk and disorderly to me. We'll hold him for Sheriff Payton, but somebody's gotta get hold of that horse."

"I've seen it before." A woman in the crowd pointed and clutched another woman's arm. "I saw it the day it dragged its rider across City Park."

She looked at Dan and Grace, at Harley again, and then back to Grace. "Her! She was the rider. She snatched a handkerchief off the ground and pulled herself back up to the saddle!"

Grace eased out of Dan's hold and walked around behind Oglethorpe. "If I were you, I'd stay right there. Unless you want to be one of the few people ever deliberately trampled by a horse. I'm sure Thorson could film your corpse after the fact."

With her voice low and soothing, she gathered Harley's reins and led him away from the ruckus.

Dan joined her, anger rising again at the sight of her blood-stained blouse. "You're bleeding. Let me help you."

Reins in hand, she swiped at tear tracks trailing her face. "Like I said before, Dan Waite, you are an artist and a gentleman, but I think I can manage." Gripping the saddle with her right hand, she lifted her left leg and looked over her shoulder. "However, since you offered …"

CHAPTER TWENTY-TWO

Grace welcomed Dan's strong hands around her waist as he lifted her to the saddle. When he stepped up behind her, lifted her again, and settled in the seat with her on his lap, she knew it wouldn't be the most comfortable ride. But she'd not change it for the world.

She'd never felt safer.

Several people in automobiles took to the road behind them—an actual parade across the Fourth Street bridge and into town. Someone made it to the sheriff's office ahead of them, and the deputy was standing out front by the time she and Dan arrived.

"Remember that cur I told you about who hit the widow Berkshire?" Grace lifted her arm and winced, revealing her blood-soaked sleeve. "You might want to ask him about his Gambler's Draw, though it's not a derringer. You'll find him in the Prospect Heights jail."

One of the filming company's green cars pulled up next to them and Thorson got out.

"Are you all right? I heard Thorpe's locked in a cell where we were going to film a jail break—"

"Yes, he is. And I won't be working on that scene if it's all the same to you." Grace lifted her arm again.

Thorson went white. "I had no idea …"

"You're right," Dan said. "You didn't. I'll be talking to the Businessmen's Association as well as the sheriff."

At the threatening tone of his voice, Grace leaned toward the director, "You missed a great shot of an angry horse today."

Dan growled something under his breath and reined Harley down the street. The parade behind them thinned out, and the clop of Harley's hooves and easy sway of his stride set Grace back against Dan's chest as he took her home.

There it was again, that word.

Home.

The boarding house sat mute, untouched by all the excitement. Dan rode around to the barn and corral, where he stepped off first and then lifted Grace from the saddle.

Unwilling to be parted so soon, she wrapped one arm around his waist. He encircled her, stroked the back of her head, and kissed her brow. She could stand like that forever in spite of the dull ache that began to throb in her arm.

When he tipped her chin up and caught her lips with his, she knew that forever would not be nearly long enough.

Harley blew, and Grace looked his way.

"What is it?" Dan turned her face toward him, concern in his eyes.

"The first time I saw Oglethorpe, he hit Dorrie and knocked her down. We charged him and chased him off. I told him if he ever tried that again, I'd turn Harley loose on him."

Dan tightened his arm around her. "I'm sure Harley remembered the encounter. He's a good judge of character."

Grace drew a deep breath. "I want to check the pasture, especially around the edges for anything that might have been thrown in from outside."

"Do you suspect someone would try to poison him?"

"Oglethorpe threatened to, and I wouldn't put it past him to have already thrown larkspur or hemlock in there. Maybe wild irises."

Dan's brows drew down and his eyes darkened to onyx. "What else did he say to you?"

"Ugly threats. Scare tactics, really, but Harley took care of him." She cupped Dan's dear face in her hands. "As did you."

"We need to get you to the doctor." He kissed the tip of her nose.

Interrupting, she pressed her fingers against his mouth only to have him take hold of them and kiss them as well as the palm of her hand.

"What if we go to the river instead of the doctor?"

That old laughing light returned to his eyes. "You're serious, aren't you?"

"Yes. It'd be good for Harley and it'd be good for my arm too. And if you have a change of clothes, it'd be good for you as well."

"Do I smell that bad?"

"No!" She gave him a shove. "That's not what I meant."

He pulled her into another kiss—hungry, searching, leaving no doubt as to what *he* meant.

~

At the river, Harley walked in unattended as if remembering his last trip to the cooling comfort. Grace and Dan pulled off their boots and stockings, and Grace left her skirt hanging below her knees rather than hike it up, a thin grasp at propriety.

They waded into the current at knee depth, and she bent to submerge her arm—sleeve and all. Cold water would wash the blood from the fabric, but it also numbed the throbbing pain. Not medicinal, but healing nonetheless. And then she remembered.

"Oh!" She touched her head.

Dan pushed through the water to her. "Are you hurt somewhere else?"

"I lost my hat. The beautiful hat you made for me."

His shoulders visibly relaxed and he gently ran his hand up and down her right arm. "I wanted to talk to you about that."

She blinked, then dropped her gaze to the dark water, watching it swirl and eddy around Harley's legs. Was he angry?

Dan moved closer, still holding her arm, nearly breathing the very air she needed.

"I'll make you another one. But this time, you won't be paying for it."

When she looked up, he kissed her tenderly, as if she were a china doll.

"Let me cover you the rest of your life."

Her heart jumped. What was he saying? Was he asking her to, to—

"Marry me, Grace Hutton. You've changed my life and opened my eyes. Be my wife and let me love you."

Wrapping her good arm around his neck, she gave him her heart in that moment, but couldn't resist taking advantage of the opportunity. "Free hats, huh?"

Quick on the draw, he scooped her out of the water and tossed her over his shoulder. "Come on, woman. We've gotta get you healed up for the wedding."

~

Dan admired the fine precision of Doc Miller's stitch work as well as his medical opinion.

"The cold water was probably the best thing you could've done for this cut." Miller tied off the last stitch and cut the thread.

The laudanum had taken affect, for Grace merely frowned and turned her head away.

Dorrie's eyes danced with unmitigated laughter, as if she was enjoying every minute of Doc's attention to someone other than herself. "How many doses should I give?"

As Dorrie followed Doc to the door, Dan bent low over Grace and whispered against her ear. "I'm going to carry you upstairs. Keep your arm in your lap—I've got you."

Eyes closed, she turned her head and a faint smile brushed her lips.

Someday soon, he was going to carry her upstairs again, but it wouldn't be for recuperative reasons.

Gently, he slid his arms beneath her shoulders and knees, then lifted her to his chest. He'd best keep his thoughts tethered.

He toed open the door at the head of the stairwell. The star quilt had been returned and folded over the foot of the bedframe. He laid her gently against the pillows and draped the quilt over her.

Smoothing her hair from her brow, he leaned close. "I love you, Grace. Now and always."

Her blue trunk sat in one corner, upright and open, and on the left side hung what looked like clothes from her performing days. A silk blouse and red velvet skirt with cutout design, and on a small shelf, a pair of beaded, white-leather gauntlets.

What had brought her back to Cañon City? Heartache? Homesickness? Whatever it was, he thanked the good Lord for His timing.

He pulled her door partly closed and returned downstairs. Pop and Dorrie sat at the kitchen table playing checkers and drinking coffee. The sight of them tightened his chest. More of God's timing, and just what his father needed—a woman's touch and companionship. Someone fussing over him who wasn't his son.

Dorrie Berkshire was more than Dan had dared pray for.

An idea hit him as he crossed the threshold. "What would you think of turning the porch room into a bathing room? That way you wouldn't have to leave the house and walk all that way in the winter."

Dorrie looked up at him, considering what he'd said. "That sounds wonderful, Dan. But don't think you're going to add a privy onto the house. I won't have it. I can't believe some folks have included them inside their homes."

Dan laughed and paused at the end of the table, arms folded, studying the checker board. His father had two open moves, but when Dan looked at him, Pop cut a side-eye and gave a slight jerk of his head.

He was going easy on her!

"Would you be opposed to plumbing? Both hot and cold?"

Dorrie's hand stopped halfway to her next move. "My heavens, I haven't that kind of money. What's gotten into you? And where are you going to sleep if you turn your room into a bathhouse?"

She plopped a black checker down on the board, clearly not thinking about the move.

Pop coughed, but nothing like he'd been doing that last couple of years. More of a polite substitution for an all-out belly laugh.

"Well?" Dorrie persisted.

"With Oglethorpe in jail, I might sleep at the shop while I'm working on closing in the porch. After that, I can re-assess."

By now, Pop was watching him closely. With that kind of scrutiny, Dan was hard-pressed to keep a grin from breaking out.

"What aren't you tellin' us, son?"

"Oh!" Dorrie's hand flew to her throat. "We're going to have a wedding, aren't we?"

Dan pointed out a move that would help her. "After you win this game, you can check on Grace. She might have something to say about that."

He grabbed his hat from the hooks by the door. "I'm going to the livery. See about getting a wagon for a trip to the lumber yard tomorrow morning."

The old house needed a good update, and he was happy to do it between hat orders. That included having a telephone installed. Dorrie might not agree on that count, but if the four of them were going to live there, they'd be better off in this day and age with a telephone.

As he crossed the street for the livery, he wondered how Dorrie would feel about electric lights.

CHAPTER TWENTY-THREE

Grace's head throbbed as she reached for a glass of water on the nightstand. The effort stabbed her left arm at the elbow and she jerked, knocking the glass to the thick rug beside the bed. Fully awake, she sat up, surprised to see the room completely dark. The lamp had burned out, and no light teased at the window. Dawn was yet to appear.

Memories seeped in and she laid back against the pillow, leaving the glass for later. She felt the bandage on her arm and heard again Oglethorpe's grizzly voice at her ear threatening her. Dorrie. *Harley.*

What if he had scattered toxic plants in the pasture? She hadn't checked last night, nor would she be able to see now until daylight.

Restfulness gone, she flung the quilts back and set her feet on the floor, gasping at the wet rug beneath her toes.

Later. Later she'd take the rug out and mop up the spill. Right now she had to get to Harley. Something urged her to hurry.

She dressed as quickly as she could with one arm nearly useless, struggling most with her boots. Not taking time to braid her hair, she brushed it out and let it hang loose.

Pausing to listen at the stairs, she heard no sound from Dorrie's room. Surely she wasn't up yet cooking breakfast. Downstairs, the study door was closed, and across the hall, curled up on the pallet, Dan slept soundly. Not snoring, but with a rhythmic breathing she knew meant he was deep in sleep.

Holding her breath, she made her way back down the hall without stepping on any squeaky boards. At the back door, she pulled her hair up with her right hand, twisted it atop her head, and reached for her old hat. But why bother? There was no sun, no wind. She let her hair fall down her back and slipped out to the porch.

So dark the yard, the barn. No moon, and no pinking of the sky. What was the saying—it is darkest before the dawn?

Fall pinched the air and her coatless arms. No night birds sang, no cooing of doves from the barn. No song from any winged creature. Starlight was her only guide with the outline of the barn against a glittering sky. No breath of wind. Only stillness.

Stopping at the pasture fence, she strained to see Harley's form standing out against the trees lining the river, but no silhouette appeared. It was unusual that he would not come to her, for he had always known when she approached.

A chill crawled up the back of her neck.

Careful of her footing, she hurried inside the barn. With no matches to light a lantern, she felt her way along the alley to the first stall, then on to the second and the third which was Harley's. His scent came to her, mixed with hay and dust. Dust? Had he been pacing in his stall?

"Harley?" Her voice came small and weak in the dark, stirring her to greater strength. "Harley," she demanded. "Are you here, boy?

A low whiffle came, close to the ground. Through the window in the outside wall, starlight revealed a still shape lying in the middle of the stall. "Harley?"

She rushed through the open gate and fell beside him, hugging his neck. He blew and tried to raise his head. His feet stirred as if pawing the air.

"Oh God, no. Please, not Harley. Have mercy."

She pressed her face against his neck and stroked him. Muscles twitched beneath her hand, but he made no movement to stand.

"I'll be right back, old boy. I have to have light to see what's wrong. Don't move."

Tears pressed against the back of her eyes. What a stupid thing to say—of course he wouldn't move.

She left the stall door open and ran down the alleyway, across the yard and up the ramp. With no worry about making noise, she flipped on the kitchen light and grabbed the matchbox from the stove.

"Grace." Groggy and deep-throated, Dan stood in the doorway. "Why are you up? What's wrong?"

Hearing his voice set her tears free, and she faced him but didn't stop. "It's Harley." At the door she paused. "He's down in his stall."

"Down? As in lying down?"

"No, he's down. Something is wrong but I can't see, so I came back for matches."

"Wait and I'll go with you. Let me get my boots."

"I can't wait, but come. Please come."

She ran to the barn and grabbed the first lantern she came to. From there she found others, and lit them, setting them at intervals along the alleyway and in Harley's stall.

He gave no notice of her approach.

Her throat closed off and she dropped beside him.

His breathing was labored.

"God, please. Help us. Tell me what to do."

Dan knelt beside her, pushing her hair back over her shoulder. "When did you find him like this?"

"Just now—moments ago—just before I ran to the kitchen."

In the lantern light, worry creased his brow and the mirthless set of his lips.

"Pray, Dan. Please pray. I can't lose him…"

Her voice broke and he drew her into his arms as she wept. Tightly but gently he held her, and his voice was deep and beseeching as he asked for God's help. For wisdom. For a miracle.

She wrapped her arms around him and held on.

Fingering hair from her face, he smoothed it back. "You mentioned Oglethorpe's threat."

She sucked in a breath and looked around the stall as if the cur was in the barn with them. "We didn't have a chance to check the pasture. And we can't see it now. What do you suggest?"

"We didn't put him up last night, we left him out. How'd he get in here?"

"A stall on the other side connects to the pasture. I leave that gate open as well as this one. He can walk right in."

"Could he have gone back down to the river, gotten into something there that would make him sick?"

Grace slowly shook her head, numbed by the horror of what was happening. She couldn't think, couldn't focus.

"Is there a vet here?"

His question broke through the haze. "I don't know. Most of the ranchers tend to their own stock. Smitty does the same at the livery. I don't know if a vet has come in while I was gone. My grandfather helped in that way years ago. In fact, he helped my grandmother's mare foal—"

Grace's head lifted and she looked toward the house.

"What?" Dan pushed upright.

"The study. His books. The bottom row has veterinary books."

~

Dan eased the study door open with a glance at Pop.

Still sleeping.

As quietly but quickly as possible, he lit the lamp from the desk and knelt before the books on the bottom shelf. Only a handful of them had to do with animal husbandry and veterinary medicine. Several pamphlets and smaller books addressed broken bones, shoeing, training.

"God, I need wisdom," he whispered. He didn't have time to read everything.

Reaching for the bigger book, he sat back on his heels and ran a finger down the index, poisons … toxins … toxic weeds …

"What are you looking for?"

His father's voice came clear and steady from across the room.

Dan stood, surprised to see Pop braced on his elbows, watching him like an owl on a tree branch.

With a sigh, Dan fingered through his hair. "Grace's horse is down and we don't know why. Her grandfather was a horse doctor as well as a preacher, and I'm looking through his books. Trouble is, I don't know what I'm looking for."

"How is the horse acting?"

"He's just lying there, labored breathing."

"Can you hear his stomach? Is he twitching or kicking?"

"He doesn't act colicky. But Grace said that Oglethorpe fella threatened to poison him. We didn't get a chance to check the pasture last night. Or the barn."

Pop pushed himself to a sitting position. "We had a horse get ahold of larkspur once. Typically, they don't eat it, but it's a possibility. So is staggerweed."

"I remember that. We gave her lots of water, worked at keeping her calm."

"Get him up if you can. Give him a little salt in your hand to make him thirsty." Pop swung his legs over the edge of the daybed and pulled his wheelchair against it. "I'll get some coffee on for you."

Dan held the chair steady as his father got himself into it and settled.

"You go on out and help Grace. She probably needs you more than the horse does. I'll read through some of those books and holler if I find anything."

His father rolled through the doorway and down the hall. "And I'll be praying."

If only Harley could recuperate as well as his father had.

Dan grabbed the salt cellar on his way out and was met with a lighter sky. No matter how bad things got, darkness couldn't hold it back. Dawn came. Light won.

As he approached the stall, Grace's voice came to him, soft as morning, reassuring and comforting. She stroked Harley's neck, lying with her head on his shoulder and her hair splaying across her back. She sat up when he entered.

"Did you find anything?"

He held out the cellar.

"Water?"

"Yes. Let's give him a little salt and see if we can get him to drink. But first, let's get him up."

As the sky lightened, hope rose with the sun. Grace rubbed Harley's legs while Dan worked salt under his lip. The more they coaxed and encouraged, the more responsive Harley became, and when sunlight broke through the trees, he pushed to his feet, wobbly and weak, but upright.

"I'll get fresh water." Dan dumped the bucket outside, filled it at the pump, and set it in front of Harley. "Lord, we've brought the water to the horse, but it'll be You who makes him drink."

Slowly, Harley lowered his head to the bucket, blew into it a couple times, then lipped it before drinking it in.

Grace's voice broke in a cry.

"He's gonna make it," Dan said, rubbing the horse's head. "Is there fresh hay, some that's clean?"

"Yes." Grace ran her sleeve across her eyes. "I'll go through it, then fork some into the trough for him."

"Check the trough first. There's no telling what Oglethorpe did."

Grace left for the hay mow and a voice called quietly over Dan's shoulder. "How is he?"

Dorrie stood at the edge of the stall, her coffee pot in one hand and two mugs dangling from the other.

"I believe he's going to make it." Dan kept his voice low and moved slowly as he took the mugs and let Dorrie pour.

"Thank you for bringing this out. Pop must have told you what was going on."

"Your father and I know more about what's going on than you think."

At the sparkle in her eye, Dan laughed. That observation was two sides of the same glass, but he kept his opinion to himself.

"I'll be back with breakfast. Something easy to eat out here—bacon and biscuits."

CHAPTER TWENTY-FOUR

For the next week, Grace lived in the barn with Harley. Dan brought her meals and shared them with her, then went back to work either at the shop or at the house, walling in the porch room. It was to be the new bath house, he'd told her, with running water, hot and cold. Oh, the luxury!

His plan included a door through to the kitchen and installation of a parlor stove. The potbelly would stay in the shack, which he also planned to finish off for a boarder. But not this fall. Too much was going on.

And most of it was going on in her heart.

Dan had brought his cot for her to sleep on in the alleyway, and it smelled of him. Slightly, but enough to make her not want anything between herself and the canvas until the cold drove her into a wool-blanket-and-quilt cocoon. A couple of nights, she'd taken the blanket and curled up next to Harley in his straw-filled stall. He was still weak, but getting stronger by the day, and at night his warmth was enough for both of them.

She and Dan had scoured the pasture, where they found larkspur thrown along the fence line. This late in the year, there was no flower or new growth, thank God, so the toxin had been less.

They'd also cleaned all the stalls and gone through the hay—a tedious task, but worth every minute spent for Harley's sake.

Grace knew that Harley wouldn't be with her forever, though if she could make it happen she would. But with the slowly, encroaching arthritis, his days of exciting rescues were over. God had given her Harley the Wonder Horse for a season. Or perhaps He'd given her to Harley for a season of care, and rest, and a quieter end to his days.

Evenings in the barn had provided her time to think about her future, the future that God had planned and she'd had no inkling of. His words had proven true—His thoughts were indeed far beyond her own. Thoughts of a home, family, and faithful love.

On her last night in the barn, a mewling sound drew her to the open stall that connected to the pasture. As she crept up on it in the near dark, the shadow that she had seen earlier darted up and over the wall. However, part of it remained in the corner—the part that was making such a pathetic cry for comfort and warmth.

Returning with a lantern, she knelt next to a ball of mewling kittens, days old with eyes not yet open. This called for a bed of hay, and she brought a wheelbarrow full. Moving the kittens aside and filling the corner with hay, she returned five little hungry babies crying for their mother.

When Dan came with her supper, she pointed them out.

"Look what I found."

A smile warmed his face in the lantern light. "How many?"

"Five."

"Have you named them?"

Dorrie's words came to mind from when Grace had asked a similar question. *No sense getting attached to something that won't get attached to me.*

"Not yet," she said, with every intention of turning that theory around by naming them first and making sure they did attach to her. A few good mousers in the barn would be a boon. "I think I'll start with Kip, Ty, and Jay. You can help me with the other two."

"Me?"

"Yes, you. And you can start helping by bringing me a bowl of warm milk."

"They can't drink that."

"No, but their mother can. She'll get used to me handling her babies and maybe get used to my smell on their little bodies. It's worth a try."

"What's her name?"

"I think I'll call her Mama. It gives her a sense of purpose. A place to belong."

Dan sidled in against her and looped her in his arms. "I once heard you say something like that about yourself."

A quiet laugh rolled through her chest. "At the time, I was hoping you hadn't heard me."

He kissed the top of her head, her cheeks, then swept her with a look that said more than he probably realized.

Or maybe he did.

~

After making sure Harley was secure, fed, and watered the next morning, Grace took her bedroll and cot to the house and left them in the transformed porch room. Dan had walled it in, added a door to the kitchen, and set up a small parlor stove. The old tin bathing tub replaced the cot.

Amazing what forethought and skill could accomplish.

Since the tub wasn't in use, she laid Dan's collapsed cot across it with the quilts and blanket and used the new door to the kitchen.

"Good morning." Dorrie was alone, manning her place at the stove. "I was hoping you'd be in this morning before anyone else came for breakfast. I'd like to speak to you about something."

She brought two cups and saucers to the table and poured hot tea before taking her seat.

Accustomed to Dorrie not wasting words or time, Grace drew her chair out and accepted the tea Dorrie pushed closer.

"Thank you. I must admit, this is more comfortable than the barn."

"Is Harley well on the mend?"

"Yes, he is. I'm afraid his performing days are over, but I have some ideas about what will come next. That is, if we can continue to board here."

At Dorrie's momentary silence, Grace's insides tugged in dread. What would she do if she and Harley couldn't stay?

Dorrie sipped her tea and frowned, then added a spoonful of sugar. As she stirred, she cast a questioning eye at Grace.

"I'd rather you not board here."

Grace's heart sank and her jaw went slack. She raised her cup, hoping to hide her gaping mouth and disappointment.

"Is there a reason for the change? Have Harley and I been too much of a burden?"

A not-so-frail hand swatted the air. "Nonsense. I'd just rather you not rent, as it were. I'd rather you move in. Permanently."

Grace stared.

"You have been a great help to me and the companionship I needed. I was getting a bit addled, tottering around this old house by myself with no one to talk to or spend evenings with on a regular basis."

The woman was lonely. Grace rolled her lips, sealing the knowledge within her.

"We could have a partnership of sorts. Similar to what your Grandmother Annie and I had." Dorrie fussed with her faded collar and dusted her black bodice.

The thought of stepping into her grandmother's place gifted Grace with a surprising sense of worth. Never had such a thought crossed her mind.

"I am honored, Dorrie. Thank you."

"Well, dear, I understand there is to be a wedding."

Grace choked on her tea and set the cup down hard, spilling the liquid. Dorrie was nothing if not direct.

"Um, yes, I suppose so. I mean … Oh, Dorrie, I'd nearly forgotten with the worry over Harley being poisoned and my sleeping in the barn." She poured the spilled tea back into the cup, confident of the answer she was about to hear. "Who told you?"

"Hmph. No one told me. I read it all over that young hatter's face. It's a good thing he doesn't play poker." She leaned toward Grace with a concerned look and hushed voice. "He doesn't, does he?"

Laughter bubbled up and washed away Grace's unease.

"I have been thinking," Dorrie said with new resolve, "how nice it would be to have Daniel stay here as well, since his son will be moving in. The last few days with all of us together here have done my heart good." Gray eyes glistened with moisture.

"And mine." Grace laid her hand on top of Dorrie's and gave a light squeeze.

"It's settled, then. You and Dan will have your room upstairs and Daniel can stay in the study. When do you plan to be married?"

At this rate, Dorrie would keep all four of them hopping.

"We haven't talked about it. He asked only, what—a week ago?" Grace rubbed her forehead. "So much has happened so quickly."

"I understand. But I never have been a fan of long betrothals, particularly if one is past one's teen years." Another sip of tea gave opportunity for another side glance.

Grace chuckled. "I'm sure you are aware I am well past my teens. Five years past."

"Good. It's settled, then. We should have a wedding before winter—which is only months away, you know. We must get all this remodeling finished before the snow flies, and well, that could be tomorrow!"

Daniel rolled down the hallway and into the kitchen. "An awful lot of talking going on in here so early in the morning."

Dorrie rose with pink cheeks and shining eyes. "Stop your complaining, Mr. Waite. I have a hot cup of coffee and a plate of eggs for you."

Daniel winked at Grace and gave her a nod as he rolled into his place at the head of the table.

Grace had not yet made it to the parlor, so she had no idea if Dan was still sleeping.

"He's gone," Daniel said, accepting a mug of coffee from Dorrie and clearly reading Grace's mind. "Went to the lumber yard again."

Hotcakes and bacon were becoming Grace's favorite breakfast, but she excused herself after only one helping. She'd slept in the barn for a week and feared she smelled like it. A bath was priority.

"I noticed the bathing tub has been moved to the porch. Is it ready for use?"

"Dan hasn't plumbed it yet, or hired someone to do it, but there is a drain." Pop buttered his second stack of cakes.

"There's a full kettle on the stove out there," Dorrie added, "and the little stove's firebox is full of kindling. It won't take long to heat the water."

"Thank you, Dorrie, for another wonderful breakfast, but I have errands to run this morning, so I'll get the fire going for a bath and afterward clean up these dishes for you."

Daniel shook his head. "No need. She's got me drying china now. You go on to town."

Dorrie blushed and hmphed, and Grace took her dishes and tableware to the sink. "Thank you, Mr. Waite. Would you like me to pick up some Oreo Biscuits while I'm in town?"

"Only if you call me Pop. I hear we're about to become family."

Grateful her back was to the table, Grace blinked quickly, stifling the gratitude threatening to spill down her face. The four of them were already family.

~

During the long, dark nights in the barn with Harley, Grace had formulated what she wanted the flyers to say:

Children's Riding Lessons

Must Provide Own Horse or Pony

~Experienced Instructor~

Inquire at Berkshire Boarding House.

The pressman at the *Record Newspaper* was more than happy to set the type for her, and he offered to add a plate of a young boy and girl with a saddled pony. The flyers would be ready in two days. She ordered enough to post at the grocery, the general, soda fountain, feed store, Dan's hat shop, and a few other places.

She had not yet decided what to charge and considered working out fees with each individual family. Expense should not keep any child from learning something so important and joy-filled as horseback riding. But they had to bring their own horse, hence the qualifier. She knew a horse was only as good as its rider, and she wanted to teach both of them to work with each other.

At the grocery, she picked up two tins of Oreos and a bag of peaches from a local orchard. The smell was delightful, and on her walk home, she held the paper bag directly beneath her nose.

Only one errand remained undone. A wedding dress.

With all her independent thinking, living, and refusal to blend in with the status quo, Grace had not given much thought to the latest fashion in wedding dresses. She'd prefer to wear her fringed riding skirt, but that would not show what the occasion—and Dan—meant to her.

She refused to return to the dress shop, but the General had a Montgomery Ward catalogue. She could go back for a quick look. Did Dan have one at the hat shop? Maybe she could borrow it and look through it privately. She had no sisters to share such a decision with, but—

Crossing a side street, she stopped mid-step and mid-thought. It had not occurred to her until that moment. She had sisters-in-law. And one was a seamstress. Of course.

The horn of an impatient automobile driver scooted her on her way.

Grace had been gone longer than she intended, and dinnertime was not far off. She hurried up the front steps and into welcoming warmth, pausing briefly by the parlor fire. Leaves would fly soon, and she and Dan must decide on their wedding day. If she tarried much longer, theirs would be a December wedding, like that of her grandparents, Annie and Caleb.

Low voices floated along the hallway from the kitchen, and Grace headed that way, but stopped suddenly at what was unfolding before her.

Dorrie held her oversized coffee pot above Pop's mug on the table. He rolled his chair back, and she looked up in surprise.

As if watching a tableau come alive before her, Grace could not take her eyes from Daniel Waite as he gripped the armrests of his chair and pushed to his feet.

Dorrie stood rooted to the floor, one hand holding the pot, the other at her bodice.

He took the pot from her, set it on the table, and pulled her into his arms, wrapping them around her and cradling her against his chest.

Dorrie began to cry.

Grace wasn't far behind, and her vision blurred as tears brimmed. She backed into the parlor, unwilling to disturb the miraculous moment, but in the stillness, she could make out his voice.

"Dorrie Berkshire, you have resurrected me from a painful existence. Since I've been staying here in your boarding house—no, even before that—I have believed that we need each other. I love you. Would you consider being my wife?"

Grace clapped a hand over her mouth, fighting to keep her emotions inside and hear Dorrie's reply at the same time.

A long moment passed before her spry answer came. "I thought you'd never ask," she said. "The sooner the better."

Grace was going to choke to death, right there in the old parlor, she was certain of it. Marshalling all her resolve, she squelched her rising laughter, reset the shopping bags in her arms, and stole into the study. Setting her bags on the desk, she pulled the heavy scrapbook from a shelf and sat down with it in her lap.

She knew exactly where to turn to find the picture she wanted—one of three happy couples on their wedding day. Looking again at her grandmother Annie, she saw herself in the woman's eyes.

Grace understood the joy of sharing a wedding day with others in addition to her husband. She couldn't match the photograph person for person, but who better to have join Dan and herself than his father and Dorrie Berkshire as they exchanged their vows.

CHAPTER TWENTY-FIVE

Smitty named a fair price for the buggy and mare he'd been renting, but Dan needed something bigger. His responsibilities had grown to include more than his father.

Dan was about to be married.

And take on a family of four.

And if he had his way, that number would soon grow to include children.

Three months didn't seem like enough time for so many changes in a man's life, but the Lord didn't necessarily work on man's schedule.

The harness shop on Main Street gave him the name of a man who had recently purchased an automobile and was looking to sell a double-seated buggy. Dan worked out a deal that included hats for the man's entire family and ended up with a horse and carriage to seat four.

His first trip was visiting the ranch with Grace so she could talk about the wedding with her brothers' wives. Hopefully, the brothers would be there. Dan wanted their blessing on his intention to marry their sister, but if they didn't give it, well, that made no bit of difference to him. Grace Hutton was an independent adult who had agreed to marry him on Saturday, 7 December 1912.

Two weeks from today.

And this morning, she looked as beautiful as a bride walking down the ramp toward the waiting buggy. She stopped first at the mare with apple slices, a good neck rubbing, and private words between woman and horse that Dan would never know. He chuckled.

It didn't matter, so long as she loved him. And she did.

"This is a very handsome carriage, Mr. Waite." Offering her hand for his help, she stepped up to the first seat and took her place.

"You have excellent taste, soon-to-be Mrs. Waite. I complement you."

Her laughter spilled over him like the morning light, and they were off to the ranch.

~

Grace scooted close to Dan as they trotted through town. This ride to the ranch was his "dry run," as he called it. Something he said firefighters in Denver did to practice for real fires. No water. Perhaps Dorrie and Pop were the water they weren't transporting today.

"You warm enough?"

The heat in Dan's eyes made her plenty warm, but she kept that to herself. "Yes. Thank you for bringing along the quilts."

"There's a foot warmer with hot coals inside." He leaned over and looked under the bench. "Right behind you down there. You can pull it out, set your feet next to it, and wrap everything with a quilt."

"What we need is a buffalo robe." Cody's troupe had several. Most were his, aside from those belonging to the plains tribal chiefs that had traveled with the show.

How far away those days seemed now.

After leaving town and starting the climb toward the ranch, the temperature dropped and clouds built up over the western ridges. Not a storm warning, merely nature gathering its blankets for colder weather.

Aspen huddled bare and white along the creeks and clung to the edges of pine forests, a sure sign that winter was near. So was her wedding, and she hoped today's visit would be profitable in that regard. She didn't need fancy, but she did need a dress. Hopefully she hadn't waited too long.

As they drove into the yard, the ranch dog ran out to greet the new conveyance. Old Tug rode drag, trailing behind. His muzzle was peppered with white, and he favored one leg. Poor old man had to be at least twelve, but his eyes were still clear and his tail still wagged.

The boys came next, bounding out from the back door to see who was driving up in a fancy carriage. When they recognized Grace, the hollering began.

Helen welcomed them as graciously as ever and put on a second pot of coffee. Mary introduced Ella and her twins, and Cale and Hugh soon came in from checking fence. Their welcome dispelled Grace's reluctance, though she fully expected them to put Dan through his paces. A dry run, so to speak.

Her money was on Dan.

Grace couldn't remember when so many people had been in the ranch house at one time and she suddenly missed her mother more than she had in years. Papa too. But time had changed so many things, including her. She was no longer the pig-tailed, tag-along little sister.

"All right boys, make yourselves scarce."

Grace had put a bug in Helen's ear about needing a wedding dress, and the woman jumped on the chore like a duck on a June bug.

"We've got things to discuss and if you don't find something to do outside, I'll have you darning socks and washing long-johns." Helen still ruled the roost.

All the men left—short and tall—and Grace quickly warmed in the welcome of her brothers' wives. Weddings and romance had a way of drawing women together, and soon magazines were strewn across the dining room table with dress patterns, coffee mugs, and a plate of Helen's gingersnaps.

An afternoon of looking through copies of the *Lady's Home Journal* with Mary and Ella gave Grace a better idea of what she wanted and didn't want. She refused a long train—nothing that would tangle her feet. Gloves were out of the question, and out of style, according to Ella, owner of the magazines and former seamstress for Selig-Polyscope. Between the three of them, and with Helen's input, Grace's dress would be a creamy silk sheath with minimal lace and straight, elbow-length sleeves. She left all the frippery to Ella's discretion.

The men returned in time for dinner, and everyone crowded around the dining table. Grace watched Dan closely and detected no tension between him and her brothers, until Hugh asked why he'd bought such a fancy rig.

Silence fell upon the room and even the clank of tableware was hushed.

Dan spread apple butter on his biscuit and took a bite, holding everyone's attention. "The way I see it, my father and the widow Berkshire are well past their horseback riding days, and I'm not too keen on either of them driving off in a buggy on their own. Personally, I'd prefer to have a good saddle horse, and I might look for one come spring. But for now I have a family of four to think of, and this 'fancy rig,' as you call it, fits the bill."

Helen gathered her dishes and stood. "Beats that farm wagon six ways to Sunday, if you ask me."

"It's not six days to Sunday," Kip said. "It's only one. Tomorrow's Sunday."

At everyone's laughter, Kip's ears flamed beet red. Dan leaned close and whispered something that made the boy smile. From the look on his face, Kip would follow Dan to China and back.

Hugh wiped his mouth on a napkin and pushed from the table. "At least you didn't get one of those rattletraps."

"It may come to that, but I intend to hold out as long as possible." Dan cast a glance her way and winked, so like his father with Dorrie.

Cale's blue eyes cut to his wife, then Hugh, and Grace. "Next spring, we might have a couple of saddle horses for you to look at. I'm thinking we could work out some sort of deal between hats and horses."

After clearing the dinner dishes and setting the boys to washing and drying, Helen loaded down Grace and Dan with jams and cookies and jars of soup. This time, Grace had a safe place to put it all, grateful for Dan's "fancy rig" choice. But in her busyness of loading, making arrangements with Ella and Mary regarding fabric and fittings, she nearly missed Kip's woe-begone stance beneath the cottonwood swing tree.

"Give me a minute with Kip," she said to Dan while he checked the mare's harness.

He led her around to the other side of the buggy and, with a smoky look, pulled her close.

"I'll give you anything you want if it's in my power to do so." He kissed her until her knees weakened, then pulled back enough to speak. "And if it's not in my power, I'll find a way."

Dan Waite was most definitely not most men.

Grace gathered herself and joined Kip at the tree.

"So how's it going with your roping?"

"Really wanna know?" Looking neglected, he slid a glance her way, testing the waters.

Her heart tugged. Such a familiar tactic from her childhood. "I really want to know. Show me what you've got."

She stood back and crossed her arms while he pulled out the cotton cord that he'd stuck down his trousers.

Smoothing out the cord and coiling it afresh, he threw it into a spin and began to step in and out, in and out, just like she had shown him.

Clapping and cheering, she ran up to him. "You've done it. I'm so proud of you!" With a big hug, she picked him up and spun him around before setting him on his feet again.

"I knew you could do it."

His face nearly split in two with a grin. "Jay and Ty want me to show 'em how to do it but I don't want to."

Oh, how familiar the feeling. "You don't have to show them everything you know. Not all at once. Pick one thing and share it—like I shared it with you. And I'll teach your more tricks."

"Promise?"

The hope in his eyes nearly did her in. It was as if he was living her life all over again.

"I promise. It will be our special deal."

She held out her hand to shake on it, and he slapped his palm against hers with a hearty seven-year-old grip.

"Deal."

Grace turned to find Dan leaning against the buggy, arms folded and one boot cocked up behind him on a wheel spoke. No impatience about him, but an easy, peaceful smile. "You'll make a great mother."

Her face warmed and she ducked her head as he handed her up to the seat.

Light fell fast on their way home, and Grace bundled herself in the quilts and blankets and scooted as close as possible to Dan. "Do you think your father and Dorrie are doing all right without us?"

He chuckled deep in his chest and the vibration worked through his arm and into hers. "They're probably glad to be by themselves for a change."

The mare's easy gate set a rhythmic pace that had Grace close to dosing in the dusk. "Hmm."

Dan raised his arm and pulled her close against him, kissing the top of her head. "Why didn't you stay at the ranch when you returned? Move in with your family rather than coming to town?"

"There wasn't enough room." She snuggled against him, aware only of his warmth and the rocking of the buggy. "But there was plenty of history, and I needed a new story. Not a rehashing of the old one."

For a long moment he said nothing, then made a sweeping left turn that she knew took them off the ranch road and onto the road to Cañon City.

His voice came soft and low, as comforting as the quilts around her. "I'm glad the Lord brought you back to town. I can't imagine my own story without you in it."

~

December blew in snowy and white, and the changes continued.

Ellen and Cale braved their way into town with the babies, bringing Grace's finished wedding dress and Cale's brawn to help Dan rearrange furniture.

The daybed from the study was stored in the former bath house, and renovation there was delayed until spring. Dorrie's brass bed came downstairs into the study that would belong to her and Pop. Her dressing table and armoire also came. The folding screen remained, joined by Grace's bed and dressing table, for that room was to be hers and Dan's.

Pop's spindle bed from the hat shop's back room was moved into Grace's former room, while the spare room remained unchanged and housed Ella, Cale, and the babies during preparations for the wedding.

Dan arranged for a telephone to be installed, and an icebox showed up one day with a big red bow on top. Grace and Dan's wedding gift to his father and Dorrie.

Grace presented Dorrie with her new dress, insisting it was an early Christmas gift, and she had to bite her lip to keep from tearing up at the look on Dorrie's face. It must have been years since the little woman had worn a new dress.

On December 6, Grace picked up the flyers and arranged for the newspaper's photographer to come to the community church the following day at ten a.m.

That evening, Dorrie and Grace tried on their dresses for Ella to make last minute alterations.

"I brought my camera along," Ella said as she tucked and pinned, "and I want to take pictures of you both tomorrow if you don't mind."

"I didn't know you took photographs." Grace smoothed the folds in her skirt, amazed that Ella possessed such skills. "Would you take one of all of us after the wedding? I've asked the *Record's* photographer to take a photograph tomorrow, but I'd love to have you take one as well."

"I'd be happy to," Ella said around the pins she held between her teeth.

"I look like a parrot." Dorrie studied herself in the dressing table mirror.

Ella laughed and pinned the waistline a bit smaller.

"You do not," Grace insisted. "You look lovely. Daniel will be beside himself."

And that was exactly where he was the next morning at the bottom of the stairs as Dorrie came down in her new forest-green dress.

Grace hid her dress beneath a lovely cape that Ella had brought, and the four of them, plus the babies, rode to the church beneath a bright blue December sky.

So many people came for the occasion that Grace had to search for Helen, Mary, Hugh, and the boys. Buffed, polished, and plastered down, the three littlest Huttons sat as still as soldiers on the second pew.

Dorrie and Pop were the talk of the gathering, he in his best clothes that fit a little loose, and Dorrie as pretty as a picture. There had been no cheek-pinching this morning, for the widow had bloomed beneath the second touch of love.

At the back of the church, Grace removed her cape, feeling a bit strange but also quite elegant in Ella's handiwork, and she heard the approving murmurs of women in the closest pews. But what overtook her thoughts and wonderings was the handsome man at the front of the church in his new vest and string tie, standing tall and proud between his father and the pastor. The mysterious cowboy who had appeared so unexpectedly in her life was here to stay.

The organist began to play, the congregation stood, and Grace and Dorrie made their way up the aisle together as Dan helped his father rise from his wheelchair. Whispers rippled through the crowd, but determination won the day as Pop reached for Dorrie's hand and tucked it in his arm.

Dan held out his hand for Grace, and with the surety of love and the promise of a shared future, she entwined her fingers in his and took her place beside him.

Two brides, two grooms, not exactly like her grandmother's wedding, but close.

As the pastor began the ceremony, memories rushed in—step-like increments that had led Grace to this day. Looking back she could see that the Lord had been with her the entire time, preparing her, preparing Dan.

And as if her grandmother Annie had spoken the words herself, Grace knew that the next—and truest—adventure was about to begin.

EPILOGUE

Two boys in denims and three little girls in trousers sat along the corral's top rail, each bundled in a heavy coat and wool cap. They were oblivious to the crisp January weather, expectation filling their eyes and no doubt fluttering in their stomachs. Grace saw herself in them—wanting to learn, wanting to excel.

"How many of you are here to learn how to ride?"

Five hands went up.

"How many of you have ridden before?"

Three hands.

"My pa said I had to learn how to do it right or he'd never let me ride again." The boy looked doubtful of his prospects.

"Does your pa ride?" If he did, Grace wanted to get her hands on him for not helping his own son.

"He rides in a buggy."

One of the other boys snickered, and the girl next to him jabbed him with her elbow.

"All right, then." Grace directed their attention to the six horses at the end of the corral, all standing without saddles or bridles and blowing white clouds from their nostrils.

"We're going to learn from the ground up, as they say. We'll start with catching your own horse—don't worry, I'll help if needed. Then we'll learn how to groom it, bridle and saddle it, mount correctly, and ride around in this corral before graduating to the pasture."

All five youngsters sat up straighter, as if trying to make a good impression.

"It will take time, so don't get discouraged. I have confidence in you."

They looked at each other and shrugged, doubtful, she suspected, of what *confidence* meant.

"That means I believe in you. I believe that you will work hard at learning how to ride until you get it. No matter what."

The boy with the buggy-riding papa gave her a big smile.

"Before we start today—" Grace whistled a low, clear note, and Harley turned out of the band and ambled to her with that running-walk, his chocolate coat shining like brown satin. When he stopped beside her, she pulled her fingers through his creamy mane and secretly signaled him into a bow.

The children cheered and clapped.

"First, let me begin by telling you a story about Harley the Wonder Horse."

~~~

Thank you for reading *Covering Grace,* the final book in the ever-popular, six-book series, The Cañon City Chronicles. If you enjoyed Grace and Dan's story and would like to read more about Grace's grandmother Annie, check out Book 1, *Loving the Horseman.* Follow the family saga through three generations of Huttons from 1860 to 1912.

For purchase links from various merchants and information on all my books, visit my website at www.davalynnspencer.com. Stay up to date on my releases and receive a free historical novella when you sign up for my quarterly newsletter. From the website you can also access my free, weekly, inspirational blog.

I would truly appreciate a brief review of this book on your favorite review sites. Please invite your friends to read this series as well as my Front Range Brides series and other books.

Thank you again.

Davalynn Spencer
~~~

The Cañon City Chronicles

Loving the Horseman

Straight to My Heart

Romancing the Widow

A Change of Scenery

Hope is Built

Covering Grace

ACKNOWLEDGMENTS

Many thanks and great appreciation go out to Tom Hirt, "Hat Maker for the Movies," who shared the fine skills and insights of a hatter; nationally renowned trick rider and instructor, missionary chaplain Linda Scholtz of Boone, Colorado, who can show you how it's done; Cindy Richardson, fellow worshipper and horsewoman extraordinaire for her knowledge of the Rocky Mountain horse and horses in general; amazing editor, Christy Distler of Avodah Editorial Services; my husband, Pastor George Casias, for traveling with me on this book journey; and to the God of hope and my King, Jesus Christ, who fills me with all joy and peace in believing and writing.

Special appreciation goes to the real-life Harley, whom I was blessed to ride. Owned by Lynn Mcnelly and adopted by Cindy Richardson, Harley will always be our Wonder Horse.

About the Author

Internationally acclaimed novelist and Will Rogers Gold Medallion winner, **Davalynn Spencer** writes historical Western romance set along the Front Range of Colorado's Rocky Mountains. She is a *Publisher's Weekly* and *ECPA* bestselling author, and an award-winning rodeo journalist and former crime-beat reporter. She teaches writing workshops, plays and sings on her church worship team, and loves bacon and chocolate—but not necessarily in that order. Connect with her at https://www.davalynnspencer.com.

~May all that you read be uplifting.~

Made in the USA
Monee, IL
11 October 2024

67041740R00125